STO

The Shining Pool

The Shining Pool

by Dale & Danny Carlson

Atheneum   1979   New York

LIRBARY OF CONGRESS CATALOGING IN PUBLICATION DATA

Carlson, Dale Bick.
The shining pool.

SUMMARY: Teenaged Ben is the only person to realize
the dangerous meaning of the underwater light
which has affected the minds of the other young people
in his small town in Maine.
[1. Science fiction]   I. Carlson, Danny, joint
author.   II. Title
PZ7.C21645Sh   [Fic]   78-13636
ISBN 0-689-30614-8

Published simultaneously in Canada by
McClelland & Stewart, Ltd.
Manufactured by Fairfield Graphics, Fairfield, Pennsylvania
Designed by Mary M. Ahern
First Edition

Contents

The Shining Pool

1 : The Pool

Mostly, Ben Donald was alone. His need to be alone set him apart from the others, but it was his being apart that saved the others later on.

Alone, his mind felt clearer. Stronger. Alone, he knew who he was, it mattered what he did. That Ben had learned that a separate self was necessary to survival helped save the others, too.

Alone, even the muscles of his body felt freer to move, to expand. And that knowledge of physical freedom became important when the others began to surrender.

Weird, Ben thought later, that the last day of school should be the last normal day. That with the end of the usual disciplines came the beginning of none.

But that was later.

In this moment of crowded, noisy pleasure, the last classes spilling into corridors and out onto sunlit lawns,

4 : The Shining Pool

Ben broke away from his friends, waved back, fled. Down the road through the Maine pine forest, halfway through Athens, their three-street town. To the left, a narrow path twisted through the scrub toward the long, island-dotted lake, surrounded by mountains, and above, the cool, calm sky.

"How you doing, Ben?"

"Going sailing?"

"School out?"

Ben nodded away the small talk, wanting to be in his own space now, unwilling, almost unable, to acknowledge any intrusion.

He moved across the small, gravelly beach to the dock. Among the other dozen boats in the water was the one that, finally, was his own. It seemed to Ben as if he had been saving money nearly all his seventeen years to buy the small, gaff-rigged sloop. All his childhood he had stood on that dock, wanting to sail the lake. But not with someone else in someone else's boat. On his own, alone.

He had painted the old wooden sailboat black with brown trim. He would have liked a Lightning, to race, but they were too expensive, and the fifteen-foot Pelican suited him for now.

Ben climbed down into the cockpit. He always lowered the centerboard first because once he had forgotten and the boat had capsized. He unlashed the mainsail from the boom, hoisted the jib. With the mainsail raised, he freed his dock lines, trimmed sails, swung over the tiller, and eased off on a port tack.

The wind was perfect. With the wind and sky, the mountains over water, Ben was filled with the excitement of peace, of freedom.

He could stop thinking, get his mind off his mind, feel inside himself for more honest reactions than he got by just thinking. Trimming his main, he pushed the tiller away from him and came about on a starboard tack. She moved smoothly now, skimming the water, the motion helping to ease ordinary thoughts from his mind.

He let go.

He was nearly a mile away from Athens, not far from the cluster of islands in the center of Crystal Lake. He slacked off sails, running before the wind, working with, not against, the natural flow of things. For moment after moment, he was caught only by the sun glistening on the water, the clarity of white cloud and mountain shapes under the intense blue of the sky, and the sensation of his own body rhythm at one with the rhythm of his boat.

Ducking the boom, Ben came about on a port tack. Veering to the left, he headed toward one of the larger islands in the center of Crystal Lake. This island was Ben's own. There was nothing here for anyone else.

The island was long in shape, with coves, outcroppings of rock, heavily forested with pine and beech trees. At the near end, the water lapped a small clearing, just enough room for Ben to beach the sloop. The sunlight on the water had been dazzling, and as he moved through the undergrowth, an occasional brilliant beam of light broke through. But basically the forest was dark and cool. The pine needle floor of the island was soft, sweet smelling. He loved it all, but he loved his destination most. He was nearly there now. Only a few more yards.

But, as he often did, once near, Ben decided to delay the pleasure of going to the pool to enjoy his anticipation. He chose a large, flat rock to sit on for a while. But the moment he set down, the peace he had been feeling was unexpectedly gone.

In its place, he felt a sudden strangeness in his body. It was a feeling of being pulled at against his own physical resistance, like the gentle tug of an ocean tide, a lapping wave receding back into the sea with whatever could not pull strongly enough against it.

Ben felt his body tense slightly against the faint beckoning and then, as it disappeared, relax. Once gone, he had no sense of the direction of the pull. But the gentle sensation was too strange to dismiss, and he stayed on the rock waiting for it to come again.

And almost in answer to his unspoken question, once more there came the sudden, strange pull, still directionless but definite, still faint but insistent.

Again it stopped. Again Ben waited, and as he waited he turned toward the path to the pool.

The pool.

Ben had explored long ago all the islands of Crystal Lake, but it was this one he had made his own. Because of the pool. In the private center of this island, where the forest was thick, where little sunlight ever came through the tall pines, was a dark, silent pool, the water deep and untroubled. The bed of moss and fallen pine needles was soft to sit on at the pool's rim. It was there Ben went to rid his mind of all the worlds that flooded him, to find the deep center of himself.

For a moment he was reluctant to leave the clearing, but since always the pool helped him sort out, he began to move toward it along the pine path. Perhaps at the pool he would get a surer reading on whatever it was that was bothering him. He moved slowly, enjoying the feel of the soft earth beneath his feet, the smell of the pine needles in the warm afternoon. He caught himself several times going faster, wanting to hurry, when what he really wished to do was enjoy it slowly. Was that part of the pulling he had felt? But what did it have to do with the pool and how fast he got there?

Ben broke at last through the underbrush, wanting, expecting the dark, still water he knew so well. It took only a moment for the shock to reach him. The pool, if it was still a pool, was not the one he had known. But what had happened? His mind could hardly take in the spot he thought he knew almost as well as his own home.

Ben couldn't move, stood exactly where he was, staring at what had once been dark, peaceful water. Now, whatever it was, whatever it had become, shone with a blue-white luminescence, alive with tiny, darting pinpricks of intense light. The water, if it was still water, shifted strangely, not windblown, but as if there were some turbulence beneath.

The unearthly glow, the darting lights, the shifting water held Ben briefly, and then—and Ben felt it specifically—something pulled him forward to the very edge of the pool.

The tugging at him, the pulling, then, had come from here.

Ben remembered hot days when he had come to swim, to float on the surface of the water. But June was still too cold to think of swimming. Then why should he feel as attracted? Why did he want to just dive in?

He reached down to touch the surface, to see if the luminescence were warm or cold, the lights solid particles or motes of energy. But because for so many years, Ben had learned to draw a fine line between what others wanted of him and what he wanted to do of himself, he was conscious that something beyond himself was gently urging his fingertips toward the surface. It was a pleasant sensation, seductive, faintly exciting, full of a kind of— what? Promise?

The undulating water lapped within inches of his feet. His fingers lowered toward the shining surface. The pull grew slightly more insistent, and something in Ben shifted, responded, wanted to give in.

To give in, unknowingly, was not one of the things Ben Donald did. Ever. He jerked himself to his feet, stared once more at the pool to fix it in his mind, and took off through the forest back to his boat. Sailing back across the lake, he could feel it behind him, the pool, not just shining, but shining in him, with him, around him.

Thank heaven the wind still held. Out on the lake, Ben felt calmer. He held the familiar tiller in one hand, trimmed the mainsail with the other. Before him was the plain, normal sight of land, the dock, the homes of people he knew appearing through the trees, the familiar shapes of the dark mountains against the blue sky.

Still the faint force reached out behind him, but lessening. Don't look back. Don't feel back.

And then it left him. Free. Halfway from the island to the shore, Ben was free.

He was also free to think. Mostly about how maybe he was crazy. How maybe he spent too much time alone, how maybe it had overdeveloped his imagination. It would explain those tugs he thought he felt. Anne, his girlfriend, had once said only a third of him lived among the living, that the rest of him lived either in inner space or outer space. That was unbalanced, she said. Free and clear on the lake, Ben shook his head at himself, smiled, and took a long, deep breath of sweet, ordinary air.

Naturally, he had been mystified by the change in the pool. Naturally, coming upon it that way had given him some rather vividly imaginative thoughts about it. And naturally, his own curiosity pulled him closer, had even followed him back through the forest and halfway across the lake.

Just as naturally, he thought, he'd have to go back there. Tomorrow. And alone.

2 : Beneath the Water

Ben's sleep that night was filled with images of the pool, the luminescent glow, the tiny lights flickering, the turbulence of the water, the sense of being gently pulled, of wondering what lay beneath the surface to generate so much that was strange. The more deeply he slept, the more he sensed its—beauty.

At dawn Ben woke instantly, and with waking, pushed against the images, wanted not to think. He knew the antidote to thinking. Doing. Letting someone else's words, someone else's life, fill his head. Not being alone.

Mr. Osenko, one of the boarders who had helped Ben and his mother meet expenses since his father's death three years before, was watching the sun rise when Ben came downstairs to go out back and split wood for the fireplace in the kitchen. Mornings were still cool. Mr. Osenko, small, plump, bald, was an English teacher at Athens High School. But it was the philosophers and mystics he loved and spoke of as often as the poets and novelists.

"Virtue is not just a state of character, but is expressed in its activity," Mr. Osenko said soothingly into the rising sun, as if he had absorbed Ben's mood. "To quote Aristotle himself, 'Those who carry off the finest prizes are those who manifest their excellence in their deeds.' Putting it more plainly," the old man went on, "pleasure doesn't lie just in being good, but doing good."

Ben agreed that thoughts were useless without action. But why should Mr. Osenko discuss the necessity of action this particular morning? Uncanny that, since yesterday, everything he thought and felt and heard seemed connected, purposeful. He didn't want to know, and knew instinctively, that it all had something to do with an enormity he didn't want to cope with yet. His vision of the change in the pool.

Mr. Osenko turned from the sun to watch Ben chop wood. "I agree with Aristotle," he said. "But unfortunately I haven't any capacity. I'm not good—I drink too much—and I don't do much good—judging by my students' grades." Shrewdly noticing Ben's quicker, less definite motions, Mr. Osenko stopped what he referred to as head stuff.

"Something," he commented abruptly.

"Nothing," said Ben. They had developed a kind of shorthand talking system, as between people who get on easily together.

"Tell me when—if—you can," said Mr. Osenko,

going back into the house.

When Ben brought the wood into the kitchen, his mother was starting the coffee. She eyed him with the critical knowledge of long intimacy. "What's the matter?" she said, as Ben dropped rather than placed the wood in the bucket. "You didn't sleep right?"

Mrs. Donald wasn't the kind of mother you had to lie to. But neither was she the kind of mother who demanded your insides as the price of her love.

Ben turned and faced her. "I haven't sorted it out yet, ma, okay?"

"Okay. You want help, let me know." That was all, and he was grateful.

"Mind if I take off?" He suddenly needed to be with someone his own age, not sit through breakfast.

"I can cope," said Ben's mother. "You can weed the vegetable garden later—and spray for white flies—and here's the shopping list. Any time for any of it is all right."

Ben smiled his thanks and headed through the dim, silent front hall, out the door, and into the early morning.

Where? Who could make him feel peaceful again? Not Anne. She sensed too much, would ask questions. Ben didn't want questions. He wanted to forget for a while, to hide from the pull of the island, of the pool.

Hugo. Maybe he was the answer. You could certainly hide in the funny strangeness of Hugo's life.

At the edge of town, a large, bizarre house stood

shrouded by overhanging trees. It looked like the back
lot of a movie studio used exclusively for horror films.
Hugo's parents were full of social messages and good
causes. They were always busy at them while they left
Hugo to do exactly as he pleased in his basement room.
What Hugo pleased was to live solely on Cokes, cereal,
and bananas and to construct stereo equipment to make
noise enough to fill his silent world. From habit, choice,
whatever, he had a low tolerance for people noises, but
Ben was someone Hugo liked.

Ben pushed open the side door that led down to
Hugo's apartment; bedroom, bath, and tiny kitchen.
Down the stairs, Hugo lay sprawled on an unmade bed,
surrounded by his speakers and amplifiers and tape decks
and phonographs and, in the corner, piles of empty Coke
bottles, cereal boxes, rotting banana peels.

"Someday they're going to condemn this place,"
said Ben wrily. Unless he had to go to school, Hugo
didn't even bathe. "You know," said Ben, "the aroma
down here is getting pretty catchy."

"I like it," said Hugo. "Rottenness suits me. Hey,
I taped six birdcalls and four new motor sounds yesterday," he added, pleased with himself. "Want to hear?"

Ben nodded and reached for a Coke and a banana
from the enormous supply on Hugo's desk.

He didn't wince as the motors and birdcalls rocked
at full volume off the walls. In fact, he invited the sounds
to invade his mind, to displace his thoughts.

Suddenly, Hugo sat up, turned down the volume.

"Why aren't you holding your ears and making faces? You know you hate this crap—and loud noises of any description."

Ben smiled at the colorless eyes and skin that reflected the habits of his large molelike friend. "Just being patronizing," said Ben.

"Terrific basis for friendship," said Hugo.

"Paying you back for all the times you've patronized me with your genius as you armed me against the fate of a life spent in school labs."

"Exams are over," said Hugo. "What's come up you can't answer now?"

Ben's normal calm shifted uncomfortably. This was the third person he'd seen this morning, and all three had noticed, picked up something different in him. But still he couldn't be alone. The images bothered him too much. And he was beginning to be aware of the faint pull again. Toward the lake, toward the island, toward the pool. Ben had never let anything disturb his self-control, his ability to command his own actions, and when he was ready to go back to the pool, he would. But not against his will.

Now he answered Hugo easily. "Something wrong with my outboard motor. Will you have a look?"

"You mean leave my cave? Actually emerge into daylight?" Hugo felt unsafe out of his basement, and except for school and noise collecting, preferred to rot like a mushroom in the dark.

"You want me stuck out on the lake?" Ben said.

"I'll look, I'll look," said Hugo, pained. "I want to record David's jazz group anyway at noon. I'll check your motor after that."

Hugo turned up his volume and turned off himself. No use staying, Ben decided. Hugo was no help. Jake maybe then.

Jake Loring lived just off High Street. He was revving up his Honda as Ben came through the back gate. Jake's mother stood on the back porch, looking helpless. Ben wondered how two such plain people as the Lorings could have produced wild Jake. Must be a throwback, Ben figured, to some more adventurous ancestor. Possibly Attila the Hun?

When Ben appeared, Jake said nothing, simply tossed him the extra helmet. Ben took a breath, as well as his life in his hands, put on the helmet and climbed on Jake's bike. Jake took off explosively, heading for Bear Mountain. He moved the bike expertly, fearlessly, up through underbrush, over rocks, through the forested heights, until they reached a rock cliff that extended over the side of the mountain.

"I can't stand it much longer," Jake fumed. "There's nothing in this town for me. It's all too slow. I've got to get out of here, Ben, New York, L.A.—someplace there's movement. If I stay here, I'll freak out."

"So why don't you just go, the way you and Susan keep talking about?"

Idiotic question. Easier for Jake and Susan to dream of conquering the outside world than face it. Ben understood. He had struggled with some of the same fears. It was why he avoided advice giving, only explored for answers.

"You know I can't go," said Jake. "It would kill my parents."

Jake's cop-out, and they both knew it. But today Ben was in no mood for an argument.

"You're not arguing with me," said Jake. "What's the matter with you?"

Another "what's the matter."

And why couldn't he tell? Why not Hugo, Mr. Osenko, his mother, someone? The pull: he suddenly realized that for some reason he couldn't talk about it. And it also occurred to him that he was actively fighting against the magnetic effect of the island, had been increasingly all morning. He had succeeded in keeping away, so far. But he realized, with startling sureness, that he would not be able to tell anyone, anyone, of the battle inside him. Nor would he be able to resist the pull for long.

Ben and Jake sat on the rock overhang, staring out across Crystal Lake, neither saying a word, neither able to help the other.

"Bad day," said Jake finally. "Let's ride on somewhere else."

But Ben had to test his discovery about the silence, and he decided he could do that only with Anne.

He dropped the pieces of dried stick he had been cracking and stood up.

"Have to get back to town, okay?"

Jake knew to let it alone, and they rode back in silence.

On High Street, Ben ran into Lakey. She had a bruise in her cheekbone, a bandage on each knee. Cheerful, shapely, and full of appetite for everything, Lakey took out her abundant energy by working on her stepfather's farm just outside of Athens and roughhousing with her two younger brothers.

"Got to find a less dangerous hobby," said Lakey, gingerly touching her cheek and winking at Ben. "How about you?"

Lakey flirted outrageously and democratically with anything male. She equally outrageously and democratically refused anyone anything but her enthusiastic appreciation.

"A nice, lonely picnic? Tackle football? A little friendly capsizing?" suggested Lakey.

Laughter released Ben momentarily, and then Lakey was gone.

He moved on, walked the length of High Street, past the General Goods Store, Walker Hardware, Jordan Bank, Lily Violet's Women's Boutique, the garage, all the familiar signposts of his life. Strangely, they didn't seem quite so familiar, as if he were seeing it all, the things and sights of his town, either for the first or the last time. Carefully avoiding even the sight of the lake, he stopped at the Loring Drugstore for a Coke, trying for at least one single solid feeling that morning.

It was no good. He needed to be with Anne. As the pull grew perceptibly stronger, the imposition of silence more powerful, he needed someone he cared about right there. Though why he thought even Anne could help, he didn't know.

Inland from High Street, the Jordan home was large and dignified, quiet. Ben found Anne in the white, ornate summerhouse at the far end of the Jordan property in her favorite wrought iron chair before the glass table covered with notes and books.

She stood up when she saw Ben. Awkwardly, with the steel brace and the medical orthopedic shoes. She had been born with a clubfoot. Two operations had already been performed. The foot, unusually, had consistently turned inward again. A third operation was recommended but Anne had refused. It was one of the few things she and Ben disagreed about. It was true it was her body, but she ought to give the doctors a chance, for her own sake and everyone else's.

Her small, lovely face was eager as he came up. "What's the matter today?" she asked instantly.

Ben said nothing. He climbed the three steps into the summerhouse, put his arms around her and held her tight. "Nothing's the matter today," said Ben, "except the usual. Hugo seems about to bury himself alive in his basement for the summer. Jake's riding the Honda like a crazy man. Lakey's democratic feelings are overflowing with vacation time on her hands." Ben paused. "And there's always you," he finished wrily, "the biggest pain in my life."

Anne stiffened. "I won't have another operation."

"Why?" Ben's voice was gentle. "The doctor said a third operation might be the last one. No more braces, no more surgically-approved shoes. You afraid to lose your one major gripe against the world?" Ben heard his own words with some shock. He had never accused her so directly before of being responsible in part for her own misery.

She didn't respond immediately. Instead she twined her fingers as she did when she was upset. "I didn't invent that gripe," she argued. "I just don't believe those bloody doctors can fix a bloody thing. But if being around a cripple bothers you—I have my books."

"Damn your mouth," said Ben.

"Tell me, Ben . . ." He felt certain she was about to go back to what was troubling him, and he was eager to see if he could overcome the silence inside.

Only Susan was suddenly there. A pile of fashion magazines under her arm and a box labelled Lily Violet Boutique in the other hand.

"Male or female time?" Susan asked coyly, climbing into the summerhouse.

"Damn," Anne swore under her breath.

The thing that had silenced Ben all morning made him contradict what he wanted from Anne. "Female time," he said, pulling back. He kissed Anne briefly and left the field to Susan's world of fashion, glamor, and the other idiosyncrasies that sometimes amused Anne.

Ben had tried all his friends, all the ones he was close to. And to none of them had he spoken a word about the haunting vision of the pool.

He strode back up High Street towards the woods that edged the town to the north. Without thinking, he was heading for the school. When he stood in front of it, he wondered why. And then suddenly he knew. He was at school because of the lab, its equipment. Ben wished it was his own scientific curiosity that made him slip in to gather a few test tubes, sample jars, and other simple testing equipment. But it was less his own curiosity than a sense, crazy though the thought seemed, that the pool was urging him to test, to touch, to come back, to do anything, something about it.

All right. He'd face it again, try its surface, its lights, and walk away. What could a strangeness in the waters of a pool do to him?

Keep him quiet, for one thing, thought Ben. Pull him back, for another. What else?

Carrying the equipment, Ben went to the dock, made his boat ready to sail, and moved out onto the lake. Was the wind perfect on purpose? Across Crystal Lake, he headed for the long, large island, beached the sailboat in its usual small clearing among the outcroppings of rock. He moved through the pines and beeches without pausing, directly to the mossy edge of the pool.

The blue-white luminescence was brighter, the tiny, dancing points of light more radiant, more unearthly than the day before. And the pull toward the moving water—greater, he knew. He could feel the stronger magnetism. Before he could resist it no longer, Ben filled sample jars and test tubes so that he could make wet mounts back at the lab of the pool's surface substance and it's lights. Carefully placing these and the other testing equipment behind the roots of a tree, Ben knew that he was going to have to surrender, at least a little.

He neared the pool, unable to resist any longer the steady pull. He stood uncertainly at the edge and then felt himself falling, as if hypnotized, drugged.

The first shock as he sank beneath the surface was that he could breathe. Below the surface the pool did not seem to be water at all, but a substance like air only more dense. He moved downward, partly of his own volition, partly drawn by something else, but not falling as he would have in air. Suddenly, he was in pain. Not pain from a blow, but a pain that seemed to touch every nerve in his body. At the moment he came near to screaming, the pain suddenly stopped, the luminescence was gone, and he found himself in total darkness. Total darkness. Except for one thing. Far into the dark was a small round light, like a tiny moon. It pulsated slightly, expanding and contracting as if it breathed.

There was no sound. In the dark world beyond the pain, Ben sensed three things: first, the pull of the small orb of light; second, a peacefulness so seductive, so hypnotic he felt in danger of losing himself to it; and third, an awareness that something prevented him from reaching the light itself.

Ben tried with all his strength, mental and physical, to get nearer the orb. He spoke aloud, he tried what he

had read of thought transference, even physical movement. Something, some power of the light, prevented all
approach, any communication. Will against will, the
light seemed to conquer without contact, without touch,
without explanation.

The soothing, hypnotic peace passed through Ben
once more, and invitation to surrender; but he resisted,
knowing somehow that he must.

And then there was a push. He was pushed away
like one of those small particles of light, pushed in the
direction from which he had come—away, upward,
back to the surface of the pool. Passing through the
moment of pain and the dense, luminous atmosphere,
Ben was once more at the edge of the pool.

What was it all about? Why had he been drawn in,
then pushed away? There was no question of the light's
powers; he could not deny those he had already been
subjected to. What other powers did it possess? Where
did it come from, the light and the power?

And what did it want?

3 : Anne and the Light

Ben was different. He was aware of it. There were changes in the contours of his mind. It came out in his responses to people, in his behavior. He was constantly in conflict. He was no longer open and free to communicate, to do as he wished. He was limited by the new thing that invaded him.

And, as if it were a drug, he spent an exhausting amount of energy battling against the attraction of the pool.

Even so, at least once every day, sometimes twice, he lost the battle, sailed his boat to the island, and sunk into the depths of the darkness to face the soundless light. Each time he confronted it, it was the same. He tried desperately to fathom what it was, to understand it. But at the same time he resisted its call to surrender himself to its power—a power that clearly offered peace, contentment, and the fulfillment of longings he could only imagine, not put into words. Each day he tried to get close, was repulsed, and finally cast out of the pool. Yet wherever he went, the pool went with him.

"Hey, what's happening to you," said Jake on the third or fourth day. "You look like you're coming off the walls."

Ben shifted a few feet toward the hardware store, trying to remember what he needed for the boat. He knew his once straight glance had shifted uneasily under Jake's stare. An addict sensing addiction?

"I'm cool, man," said Ben, turning Jake off in his own language.

"Bull," said Jake, and immediately revved the Honda in a nerve-splitting burst of noise. "Any time you want to be up front again, find me," he added and took off.

Ben found he could not respond to Jake's concern. Rather, oddly, it only made him crave the pool. Horrified, he made the connection. He knew now what he felt down there. What some people found in drugs, he was getting from the pool—something that crowded everything but itself from his mind. So that all problems became one problem and that became an overwhelming need. It was an escape, in a way, an external security that could be offered and withdrawn, offered and withdrawn until, if he let it, the light could make him entirely dependent. That would explain his irritability, his anxious feeling of conflict. Withdrawal symptoms!

Terrific, thought Ben grimly. Only now what do I do? The idiot thing won't let me ask for help, and how do you fight something alone when you feel half insane just believing in it to begin with?

This time he laughed a real laugh.

"You feel like sharing that?" asked David, coming out of his father's hardware store and saluting Ben with a clarinet.

"Not a whole lot," said Ben, with another, more uncomfortable laugh.

"Too lowly, am I, for your superior self?" David's smile was gentle.

But the dig struck Ben. Did he seem to others to be beyond the possibility of feeling pain? The irony, of course, was that he had a problem, a big problem, and he couldn't share it.

Which made him laugh again.

"Your conversation leaves something to be desired today," said David, waving his clarinet in goodby.

No question, thought Ben. But what could he do about it? Resist as much as possible. That was all. And that was what he did. But it was a lonely life.

With no one else to talk to, he sometimes heard the voice of his dead father, remembering the way his father looked up from a book to share what he found. "Don't ever escape from being as fully human as you can, Ben, the pain as well as the joy."

Only still resisting the force as well as he could in his mind, Ben had to give in to its strength, the physical pull toward the pool. There, unless he was constantly on guard, his behavior and responses altered, and he behaved and responded, not as he wanted to, but as he sensed the force wanted him to. Which might or might not be escape from being human.

Away from the pool he tried everything that came to mind to deflect his thinking from that pull, and those demands.

Ben went to see Lakey one day at the small, run-down farm where she lived, a mile out of Athens. The corrugated sheeting over the shack glinted in the sun, and the smells from the chicken coop and the pigpen were overwhelming. Lakey's stepfather lay snoring, his sons cuddled against him, under a large lilac shrub, and Ben found Lakey alone behind the curtained-off section of the kitchen that was her bedroom.

Lakey's cheerful lack of decorum permitted her to sprawl in her slip without reaching for further cover as she called out to Ben.

"Come on in. Be nice to have company, and you're pretty good-looking company," said Lakey happily.

Lakey wasn't issuing any more of an invitation than usual, but in this new confused state, Ben felt suddenly irritable at being teased. With the irritation came the tugging thought of the pool; and to counteract it, he bent over Lakey and kissed her roughly on the mouth.

Lakey's eyes widened with surprise but not displeasure, as if she had been given something she had wanted without knowing she had wanted it.

"Damn," said Ben. "Not you, Lakey. Me. I'm sorry."

"I'm not," said Lakey softly. "Don't go."

The old Ben, if he had behaved in such an unexpected way, would have brushed it off with a grin and an excuse about his momentary inability to withstand Lakey's exuberance. The new Ben found himself half-thinking, I could bring her to the light. It would quiet her. It was a thought he rejected instantly as not his own. He had no intention of bringing Lakey to the light, but that he had thought it made him shudder slightly in the bright June day and hurry off.

He went home. His mother's mildly reproving tone said more than her words. "No wood cut? No weeding? No shopping? No nothing? It's been nearly a week you haven't done your chores around here. Guess it's after-school exhaustion? We can't afford extra help, Ben. And who's to cut down that tree limb outside the kitchen window? The next storm will crack it down on the roof."

Ben knew he could never concentrate on the work around the house in his present state so he went to the bank, withdrew half his savings, gave his mother the money.

"Take it, Ma. Hire someone for a while. I'm just not coping too well right now."

His mother took the money without comment, and he was grateful. But he knew if she had asked questions he wouldn't have answered. His mind had begun to deal

with the problem of the lab equipment he had left behind the tree near the pool. He had forgotten it again
and again, and he knew he would be unable to get it
off the island and back to the lab for testing. Maybe he
could get Hugo to retrieve the stuff. He set off at once
for Hugo's, as if it were something he had to do.

The basement was locked, and it took five minutes
of knocking before Hugo let Ben in.

"What's the matter?" said Ben.

Hugo's eyes looked crafty. "They're back. I'm in
hiding. I mean, who needs their 'clean-up-your-banana-
peels' act?"

The old Ben would have laughed with understanding, enjoyed Hugo's peculiar differentness. The new
Ben heard himself say, as Hugo led the way to his room
and locked the door, "They do have a point. It is a
little weird down here."

There was absolute silence. No tapes, no phonograph, nothing. And in the silence, Ben was conscious
suddenly of what he used to be used to, and he sat down
with a grimace on the only available space not cluttered
by Hugo's dirty laundry, garbage, electronic equipment
—the edge of the unmade bed.

"You're the one who's looking weird," said Hugo.
"Since when do you walk in here with my mother's face,
as if you were about to shell out for a one-way ticket to
a funny farm? I mean, I thought you and I liked my
quaint and unusual self."

Ben felt the growing, familiar irritation, and with

it, there was a strong visual image of a gleaming orb in darkness. "You know you get lonely down here," said Ben.

"Do I?" Hugo said quietly.

What was this new urge to *do* something about people, instead of just letting them be, Ben wondered. He'd felt it about Lakey, and just now about Hugo. It had to have something to do with the light, had to be because of the light. He could almost hear the light in his mind, saying bring them to me.

He got up and ran out of Hugo's basement. After that he tried to stay away from everyone.

Susan was in Anne's summerhouse when he went there a few days and several weakening trips to the pool later.

"I wish mini-skirts would come back," said Susan, as Ben climbed the steps.

"I wish you'd think about something else," said Anne.

"What else is there to think about," said Susan, "except clothes and Jake."

There's something else, thought Ben—but not if I can help it.

Susan, always a little in awe of Ben, left shortly after he arrived.

He glanced after her, wondering why everyone seemed so odd to him, in need perhaps of what the pool had to give.

Anne said nothing. Ben sensed, though, that she

was particularly alert to him, aware of something different. And why, after all, shouldn't she be aware. Everyone else was.

It was there about her, too, the urge to compare her with the light, to sense what the light meant for her. And for the first time he had an urge to talk about it, sensed that he could. But that would be dangerous. It was what he had fought with Lakey, with Hugo, even with himself. Yet he couldn't go on. He had to share it or break. And Anne was strong. Maybe she could help him. It would be so nice not to be alone.

Ben exchanged a long look with Anne, and strangely, for him, issued not an invitation but an order. "Come with me."

Anne nodded silently, adjusted her brace, and stood, ready to follow him. He helped her down the summerhouse steps, down Birch Street to High, and toward the dock. He lifted her into the Pelican and made ready to sail toward the long island. As always on his recent trips, the wind was right. He had only to trim the sails, steady the tiller, and all went well.

Anne, whose face usually registered a careful range of emotions, began, as they sailed across the lake, to express something Ben had never seen before. An expectancy, an excitement, a kind of wonder, instead of her usual guarded humor, half-hidden affections, the faint bitterness of the injured. Seeing her flushed cheeks, the brightness in her face, he thought he had never seen her look so marvelous. But he was frightened, too. What could cause such delight, such anticipation. Could the pool exert its force through Ben's mind on the minds of others? Since no one else seemed to have been called to the pool, he had thought of it as his own thing, a problem for him alone—to have and maybe to share— or maybe not. As perhaps an illusion cast up by his own mind. But if Anne felt it, even through him, that would mean it was not a thing only of his own imagining.

"Hurry," she said, her voice strong against the wind as if she were finally to enter into the special dream everyone dreams, the thing one wants finally to happen. "Hurry," she said again.

So it was real. Ben was pleased at this proof of his own sanity. The call of the pool was real. Not a strangeness in his own mind at all. But what would happen to Anne? He understood without question that he hadn't brought her by accident today. Would he have been able to bring Lakey or Hugo, or maybe Jake or Susan? He didn't know.

He had taken her to the island before, of course. The landing, the path, pine needled under the trees, was nothing new to her. Ought he to warn her of the change? Would it matter? He had no way of knowing what they were caught up in. And he guessed that it wasn't just himself and Anne. Maybe all of them, the whole town, were involved. And maybe even more than that. Ben, feeling cold, shuddered.

He led Anne along the path toward the pool. He wanted to stop at the flat rock they often sat on, but Anne seemed not to want to pause or to talk, only to go on, toward the pool.

He watched her at the pool's edge, she watching the shifting, luminescent water, the darting lights, leaning toward the pull.

"Don't Anne," said Ben. "Please, first let me tell you what it's like. Don't until we talk. You might— want to give in. It's been trying to do something to me. Whatever the thing is, we have to fight it. Anne, listen to me."

Anne's face was transformed. She didn't even hear Ben. The surrender he battled, she clearly wanted. With only the briefest hesitance, Anne removed her brace and sank slowly into the substance of the pool. Ben followed, to protect her if he could, to prevent the level of pain, and the sight of the pulsing orb from—what? Driving her mad?

At the level of pain, Ben saw her eyes briefly, accepting. At the bottom in the darkness, facing the tiny moon of light, Ben was disturbed. With Anne's presence, the orb of light appeared to him to grow larger, to pulsate more strongly.

He saw a first confusion, then understanding—and then a rapid acceptance in Anne as surely as if it had been spelled out for him.

And he knew why the light had grown stronger.

For reasons Ben didn't yet understand, the light had needed and managed to absorb something from Anne that it had not been able to absorb from Ben himself.

The peace in her eyes as she gazed at the light made him unaccountably angry. If he didn't want the mindless peace, why should he be so angry that Anne should want it? Who was he to judge, except for himself, whether it was good or bad? Only he knew better than that. But it was hard to think down here where the actual presence of the light confused him terribly. Get out of here. Get Anne out.

Watching Anne's body undulate, dance closer to the light than he had been able to push, worried him. He suspected a far more psychic than physical pull, and that made it harder to get her back.

He called her name. She responded only after his fourth or fifth call, coming back to where Ben remained, restrained by the light.

He carried her, back and upward to the edge of the pool.

Wordlessly, she put her leg brace on again. Moved with him across the island to his boat.

Out on the lake Ben said, "Will you tell anyone?"

Anne replied only, "I can't. At least not yet."

But daily she begged him to bring her to the island. And daily he noticed the changes in her.

Most important, she grew more serene.

She read less.

She needed him, everyone, less.

And at the end of a few days, she had stopped flaunting her leg brace in the old I-want-everyone-to-notice-this-and-dare-to-feel-sorry-for-me way. The barrier of leather and steel no longer seemed to matter to her.

At the end of their fifth visit to the island, Anne's

face was so inhumanly peaceful it made Ben furious.

"What is that thing doing to you? I know what it's doing to me. It's making me bring you there. But it's doing more than that to you. What? It prevents me from testing it chemically, it prohibits me from talking. It keeps me constantly in a battle between giving a damn and giving in to a quiet death of the mind. But what, tell me Anne, please, what is it doing to you?"

The wind was high. The June day glorious. Beating, he sailed toward the wind by alternate tacks, and the Pelican skimmed across the water.

Anne didn't answer. She rested one hand on the gunwale.

The other she held out for Ben to see. No words, only a sign.

On Anne's wrist was a luminescent patch, a ragged patch of glowing, blue-white phosphorescence on her skin.

The shining phosphorous. The signature of the orb of light. Only why on Anne? Why not on his own wrist. She answered him without his asking.

"The light gave me the one thing I've never had in my life, Ben. Peace. Without conflict, without guilt, without worrying or caring about anything beyond that floating, marvelous peace. I have a sense of belonging absolutely to something, something I can share in by just being me, without change or trying, or anything except just believing. Something I can share in, a—beyond."

Her words should have sounded all right to Ben.

About peace and belonging to something beyond the self. But they didn't. Every instinct in him felt that something was wrong.

"Ben," pleaded Anne, "please, I want to go back. Will you take me back there?" Everything in him resisted now. "Listen to me," she said, her softened voice growing stronger to reach him on a level he could hear. "It's the pool that makes my brace not matter. It's the pool that makes me—all right!"

All right? Ben felt the familiar shudder. How do you tell someone who's been in pain a lot of her life there's a wrong way to get all right?

4 : The Others and the Light

By the third week, Ben was fighting off the island the way his mother was always trying to fight off her compulsive habit of finishing everybody's desserts.

"Oral magic," his mother sighed over the last of the caramel sauce. "I read about how it's the same for alcoholics and pill poppers. It's like replacing the bottle you had when you were a baby with a different kind of comfort. I'm a compulsive eater," she said with satisfaction. "It's kind of fun knowing there's a medical label for me instead of just plump person."

I'm glad there's a label for you, thought Ben. But what do you call someone who's hung up on a ball of light he can't get rid of or explain?

"What did they tell you to do?"

"Well, for one thing, do physical things to take

36

your mind off your mind," said his mother. "That way
you don't think about it."

"And that way the chores get done, yes?"

"Couldn't hurt," said his mother.

It helped a little. Every hour Ben was awake was
filled only with discipline against going to the island.
He chopped wood, repainted window frames, scrubbed
floors—not with his usual good humor, but with a frantic push against what he craved and feared.

On the third day of that week, he went to the
Jordan house.

Mr. Jordan, who should have been in his office at
the Jordan bank, was home.

He looked white, agitated, as he answered the door.

"If anyone knows, Ben, you do," said Mr. Jordan,
leading the way to the library. "What's the matter with
Anne?"

The matter? What she had seen, he knew. And the
alteration in her attitude. But the matter?

Mr. Jordan led Ben to the library window, pointed
out toward the sunlit grassy lawn.

Anne lay on a soft white beach towel, her pale
slender body in a bikini, exposed to the sun, her steel
and leather brace in full view beside her, her scarred,
twisted foot crossed carelessly over the whole one.

Anne had been taking the brace off on the island,
but it was the first time Ben, anyone, had ever seen
Anne without jeans or a long skirt to cover her leg.

Mr. Jordan's voice was rough with emotion. "I

know it seems strange to complain about something Mrs. Jordan and I have hoped for years—Anne's acceptance of herself, her body. She seems suddenly to have stopped thinking of herself as a cripple, to have stopped—suffering. That part is great. But . . ." Mr. Jordan waved a helpless hand. "She's accepted her condition so much that she still refuses to have the last operation, the one her doctor assures me could pretty well straighten out her foot for good. She says her foot doesn't matter any more. And Ben, she's stopped reading. For days, she's been going around with that funny half-smile. And whatever her mother and I say to her, her answer is, 'That doesn't matter any more.' "

Mr. Jordan ran a hand through his hair and peered through heavy eyeglasses at Ben. For a few seconds Ben tried desperately to form a few words of disclosure, to betray the light in some way. But it was just as impossible as it had always been. Something in his mind refused to move, refused to form the words. And in that moment Ben knew he was finally, wholly committed to a battle against whatever it was out there. Nothing was going to take over in him the way it had in Anne. Others might give up, but he would not. Yet there was still no way to disobey the directions of the light in the pool, at least when it came to talking to an adult.

Exhausted by his attempt to speak, Ben could only say to Mr. Jordan, "Maybe it's my fault. I've been telling Anne for years not to wrap her whole life up behind a brace and a book." He hated getting off easy like that, but was permitted to say nothing else. "I guess I also told her to relax, and maybe she's doing just that for a while, Mr. Jordan. But I'll talk to her."

Mr. Jordan nodded. "Thanks, Ben. I'll tell Mrs. Jordan what you said. Maybe it is all just that simple."

Ben went through the French doors of the library onto the lawn.

Right, simple, thought Ben. And remembered the word as he stood shocked, casting his shadow over Anne. Under the sunlight her skin was normal. Under him, where his shadow fell, the skin had a faint glow. Paler, but like the luminous patch on her wrist.

She saw that he noticed, laughed, and changed the subject by extending her legs.

Too scrambled for the moment to cope with the worst, he tried to switch gears. "If you were just lazing around exhibiting yourself to please me," said Ben, "I'd scream for joy."

"So scream," said Anne. "And how about taking me sailing?" She smiled. "Oh, not to the island," she added, seeing Ben tense. "Just anywhere."

Ben thought it might be a good chance to talk, to talk her into fighting, not giving in to the thing that had come into their lives. So he waited while she went into the house to change into white slacks and pullover, and they went to the dock.

There were a lot of others there, their friends. Hanging around the dock, not talking or doing anything, just strangely, restlessly milling around, staring out—it seemed to him, unless he were just getting crazy on the subject—toward the long island. Jake was there, and Susan, and Lakey, and Hugo, and Jimmy and Michael, David, Janie, so many of them.

Why all the kids at the dock? Not speaking, no picnic in sight or guitars, no one getting underway in smaller craft, no obvious reason for the gathering.

Ben led Anne through the crowd to his Pelican, speaking to each of them as he moved, receiving little or no response.

"David? Janie? What gives?"

Janie moved uneasily nearer David, reaching for his hand. In his other, David gripped rather than held his clarinet. He looked serious for the first time Ben could ever remember. What had happened to David the Joker?

"Nice day," mumbled David.

"Since when do you deliver a straight line?" said Ben.

Jimmy and Michael hovered close to Ben's boat. As if they wanted to board. Both slim, athletic, Jimmy's pale blond head complimented Michael's dark brooding face, light and shadow like the sky and water beyond. The contrast struck Ben more than ever. Anything dark and light together unsettled him now.

"Got room for two more?" asked Michael.

"How about another time?" Ben said lightly.

Jimmy took Michael's arm, nodded at Ben, and led Michael farther off from the boat to leave room for Anne to maneuver herself down into the cockpit.

He took Anne sailing. The sun was glinting on the water, the wind as usual was steady, the boat moved soothingly over the lake. Anne chatted lightly about nothing, but what Ben noticed most was how closely she paid attention to the way he handled the boat, asking intent questions about the sails, the sheets, the ways to use the wind or fight it, and how to operate the outboard motor in case of no wind at all.

Ben had intended to get profound, if necessary, on the subject of selling one's soul to the devil.

Instead, he ran into the wind, let the sails go, and gripped her hands. "Anne, listen to me," he said, hearing his voice go wild, "you can't, you won't—not yourself or for the others."

Anne smiled her new serene smile.

That, and the shadows of mast, sails, clouds subtly changing the quality of her skin, nearly drove Ben mad. "That thing is stealing you, don't you understand? Whatever makes us human is what it wants." He hadn't said those words before, but he suddenly knew them to be true.

Anne went on smiling. He was helpless behind mere explanation, and it made him angry.

"I'll fight for you, I promise," he said, taking control of the boat and himself once more. "I'll fight for you every inch of the way in every way I can find." But even as he said it he knew that the same thing inside him that prevented him from talking to adults would keep him from helping his friends.

Anne's eyes glittered cold and hard for a moment before they softened gently, deceptively again. "We don't all have your strength, Ben," was all she said.

Another hour, and Anne asked Ben to let her handle the Pelican.

"A new interest in life," she said in a mockery of her old, amused tone. "If I can't dance, I can at least learn to sail."

"Sure," said Ben. It had always been hard to refuse Anne anything. Now, with the new power in her and the same power pulling at him, it was impossible.

He gave her the jib and mainsail sheets and put the tiller in her hand. He felt her gaze on him, as if it were a kind of last, fully loving moment, and then she tore herself away, took herself back from him. And with her new, suddenly self-contained ability to function, began to—what was the word—began to fly! She was on her own, relieved of need at last, full of joy, separate from anyone or anything else. Except what caused the change.

Quick at everything, Anne soon learned how to handle the boat, sails and motor, nearly as well as Ben. He taught her the three points of sailing: the direction the wind is blowing, the direction the boat is going, the way the sails are set. He taught her about running before the wind, about reaching, about sailing close hauled, of the dangers of an accidental jibe, of broaching to, of rolling. He made her tack and come about over and over again, and he explained about how to fetch, to coast after the wind is spilled from the sails.

When they docked back at Athens, their friends were still milling around. Only when Ben and Anne climbed out of the cockpit, did Ben notice a difference. Now it wasn't Ben they stared at, it was Anne. And in front of all of them, most intent, was David Ginsberg.

Anne moved quietly through the group, and all their eyes turned to follow her. Ben suddenly understood. The light, finding him difficult, had chosen Anne instead as the Pied Piper. He had fought the light, constantly refusing to bring others, straining against the light's power, wanting to negate it, undermine its strength in himself. Anne was easier material, simply because what the light had to offer, she wanted. That she wore its signature, underwent its changes, was proof that Anne was to be the light's vehicle, not himself.

She had become the siren, the temptress, the bewitcher, and he could practically hear the music of the spheres, like a bad science fiction movie, around his ears. The bells of a lunatic asylum is more like it, he thought.

He wondered grimly who was to be first.

David, coming toward Anne, seemed next in line.

Ben backed off from the group, waiting for them to separate out, and then followed David to the hardware store.

When Ben walked in, David's face was wary.

"I'm not the Gestapo," said Ben, knowing that David's parents, having lost most of their family in

German concentration camps, still had a suspicion of all gentiles. He meant it as a joke, knowing that David didn't share his parents' feelings.

"You sure?" David blurted out, and then, as if ashamed of a confusion he didn't understand, added, "Sorry, Ben."

Ben played with an idea, made a connection. Was it possible the light was able to use any weakness as some sort of conductor to itself? Anne's foot, David's Jewishness? Ben didn't know how much time he'd have with David until David's mind altered, so he talked fast.

"Hey, I need your help," said Ben. "Maybe you've guessed, maybe you already know what's going on. You have one of the best brains—"

David cut Ben off instantly. "Don't tell me. All Jews are smart. Pushy, but smart. Ever occur to you why most Jews are smart, Ben? The way we've been treated for the past two thousand years, only the smart ones survived."

Ben was shocked. The David he knew spent practically no energy at all worrying about being Jewish. "What's with you? I don't need you to analyze the Jewish question. I've got to warn you about—"

"What, marrying your sister?" David moved from behind the cash register to stand in front of the screws and bolts counter. His small, slender form hunched, his eyes nailed Ben to the wall behind him.

"Don't worry, I won't. We have to stick together, ready with packed suitcases, when you tell us to move on again."

"What on earth are you talking about?"

"Israel," David muttered. "We've got Israel now. We won't go down again. And me, I won't go down at all. I've felt something—no more battle for Jewish survival, my survival—I can be part of something else now, bigger . . ."

Janie's entrance relieved the terror of witnessing the sudden disintegration of a friend. Her attention was naturally on David, so Ben reached out and grabbed her. An ordinary exchange of words didn't seem to be much of an attention-getter any more.

"If I say—don't let him—do you know what I mean?" Ben asked.

Janie ran a hand through her close-curled hair and said, "Whatever David chooses, I go with him." Her eyes looked flatly at Ben.

"Great way for you two to solve your integration problems, by copping out," said Ben, angry. He understood, though. This way they could have each other without fighting the world—in absolute peace!

One last try, and he would leave. "Janie, it isn't too late. You've got pride, guts. Don't let David wallow in whatever this wave of self-pity is all about. You both want to go to law school, remember? You both care about the world and the people in it."

"Big words, pride, self-pity," said Janie. "Since when do you lecture, Ben?"

Ben left without a word. Right. Since when did he lecture?

Since the light. Since the beginning of his fear at

what was happening.

He stared back through the lighted window of the Ginsberg Hardware Store. Janie's arms were around David, but the gesture seemed less like love than if they were committing themselves to an agreed-upon pact. From the open window, Ben could hear Janie croon, "The hell with them—let's do what Anne promises."

Anne? When had she had time to promise? Promise what? What had she said? When? Or had she somehow been given the power to convey to all those milling around the dock this afternoon what the light had taught her—with no words at all.

Ben went down to the dock that evening. The moonlight on the lake gave him a momentary feeling of calm, and the flickering of stars, the illusion of continuity.

And then suddenly, there was the rush of an engine. A motorboat, loosed from its mooring, raced across the water, the white foam of its wake streaming away from him in the dark.

Ben leaped for the Pelican, but knew he couldn't catch the motorboat; so he decided to wait it out where he was.

He knew where they'd gone, of course. Guessing that Anne had decided a sailboat was too slow, guessing she had been told to bring someone new to the pool. From the sound, she had the fifteen-foot Starcraft from Charlie's Boathouse. Outboard motor. Held six, maybe seven. Who had she taken to the island?

Eventually Ben saw them coming back, pulling away from the long island. Anne at the helm of the motorboat—and beside her, Jimmy and Michael. The light had headed him off to David and Janie while it took the other two. Jimmy and Michael, football heroes, track heroes, only because it was what their parents wanted for them.

Sure, thought Ben, perfect first targets.

At the dock, Ben confronted all three. Anne was silent. So were Jimmy and Michael. Ben lifted Jimmy's wrist and then Michael's. Each wore the phosphorescent patch, as he had known they would.

As the boys moved on, Anne said, "Don't stop me. I have to do what I'm told to earn my own peace."

Ben blocked her path for a last second. "Are you sure? Have you been told? Are you guessing? Has—has the light spoken to you, actually spoken? Anne, you better know what you're doing, because if you can't guess what's going on, I think I can."

But she slid past Ben's grasp into the blackness of the night. And he could only watch her go, cursing the thing's grasp on him that would not let him do what he wanted to do—argue, fight, scream against what seemed an increasingly deadly takeover by something that seemed less and less human.

5 : Luminescence

They were careful of their movements at first, in order not to draw suspicion from the town. Ben watched them take to the lake in pairs, small groups, casually by day, freer at night. He himself was still unable to completely resist the compulsion of the orb, had to descend into the pool and to maintain silence except among the chosen. Why he wasn't as completely drawn in as the others, he still didn't fully understand.

Whatever the reason, he had to find it, use it. But somehow he couldn't even think clearly about it.

But until he could break his own silence, find a way to act, he could at least read, listen, watch. Once he had absorbed the shock of what was happening to Athens —amazing what a mind can accept when it has to, he thought—he wondered about the probability of its happening somewhere else.

One orb at a time? Or were there many orbs together from whatever their source?

He made constant attempts to communicate the problem. But every time he did, he was left feeling like a piece of machinery that had been jammed, a part of Hugo's electronic equipment that could receive but not transmit.

He couldn't speak of it to the adults in Athens.

He couldn't speak of it over the telephone when he called people he knew outside of Athens. He sent telegrams. There were no answers. Were they even sent or received?

Every day, he tried to get out. The steering went out of control in a car he "borrowed," and he rammed into a tree two miles south. The train that hadn't had an accident in anyone's recent memory derailed the morning Ben rode on it. When Jake's bike ran out of gas, Ben realized how completely the light had cut him off. And he didn't dare travel unprotected on foot in case, as he suspected, there were other lights out there to draw him in.

But he could and did dig into recent editions of the Athens newspaper. He talked to people who came through town from other places. He listened to the news broadcasts on his radio, watched the television set. If the situation in other places was the same as in Athens, he guessed that there might not be obvious announcements of trouble, but there might be clues, suggestions that life on earth was out of joint.

But the cutoff from the outside world remained

complete. No clues from the outside world; no way he could get word out.

He felt frustrated in everything he tried, because he wasn't making much progress in changing things in Athens, either. All his friends continued to visit the light, and he could not fight against it.

Ben hated it. His friends were living in a state of increasingly peaceful release, but they were like zombies, like people who receiving more and more of some strange drug.

Ben was compelled by the light but unable to make it communicate with him directly. The others—and he could only sense rather than know it—received more direct and powerful communications from the orb. Without their more perfect communication, Ben could only observe externally and analyze things with his mind in an attempt to discover what the light was and why it had come.

What got him most was the ability of the light to keep him from interfering. He was powerless to stop Anne, powerless to prevent her from bringing everyone under the age of eighteen—the age limit was obvious by the end of that first week in July—to the island.

"Something is making that boy cranky," said Lily Violet, the silly, frivolous woman who owned the only fashion boutique in Athens. She had come to board recently with the Donalds.

Ben's mother warned him with a precise kick to the shin under the breakfast table. Don't be rude to a boarder. We need the money. Ben wished he could translate everyone as easily as he could his mother.

"He walks around as if there were a storm cloud over his head," Lily Violet rattled on. "No talk, no smiles, no jokes anymore. What's the matter with him?"

She was a poor silly old soul, but what she said struck Ben hard.

Why, if someone as unthinking and unfeeling as Lily Violet had noticed changes in his behavior, why hadn't the adults in town noticed and said something about the way the other kids were changed. Even Mr. Jordan seemed unconcerned now. Was it the light? But how? Why? How had the light erected a wall between the generations and for what purpose?

As Lily Violet picked at her breakfast fruit, Ben felt his mother and Mr. Osenko stare at him warily. Of course they'd noticed. And if they hadn't spoken, Ben knew it was because neither made silly conversation and were somehow prevented from reaching him on a more serious level. He understood instinctively that this must be true of every adult in town. He felt more isolated than ever. But after Lily Violet had blundered in, his mother made a small attempt to say something when the two of them were alone in the breakfast clutter.

"Things are bad?" she commented. Her tone was uneasy, as if she had to pick her way carefully.

"Things are bad, ma," said Ben, finding that he, too, had to strain to get out words to her at all.

"Can you cope?" asked his mother.

"I'm not sure," Ben said, leaning against the kitchen sink.

His mother concentrated on peeling vegetables for lunch as if she had to cheat by doing something else as she talked. Even then her talk was roundabout.

"When you were eight, you tamed a wild fox who had been eating our chickens by being good to the fox, by understanding the fox better than the chickens. Your father said, 'My son, he can cope with anything.' "

Understanding the fox better than the chickens. The memory caught Ben. He had learned his first lessons about the fox by first observing closely the chickens' reaction patterns. Meaning, of course, that if he couldn't get closer to the light, didn't dare give in enough to let it communicate with him, he could at least track as many reactions as possible among his friends.

Mr. Osenko appeared in the kitchen doorway. "A good point," he said eagerly, though his voice showed a strain. He too wanted to help, and by the bright look in his eye, Ben knew he had found a way of talking without direct communication. His mother had managed under cover of concentrating on something simple, physical, making use of childhood memories. Mr. Osenko now simply blurted out a quote from their common reading.

" 'I know when one is dead, and one lives.' " said Mr. Osenko, his round face bright with insistent meaning.

Ben burst into laughter in sheer relief at the cleverness of the quote, *"King Lear,* Act V, Scene iii," he responded with the intense gratitude of someone who has found a thin opening out of a prison of total isolation.

The single line from Shakespeare's play underscored his mother's advice. Seek out those who knew the light best, learn from them. But who should he choose to study? His father had taught him that the more important the decision, the more simple the solution must be. The most simple standard Ben could think of was the most obvious: the frightening alteration of the skin. It wasn't particularly visible to those who did not know it existed. The light and shadows had to be just right. And you had to be looking for it with the special knowledge only the young people had. But it was a perfect standard for the pecking order of trouble.

"I'll start coping now, ma," said Ben. "And thanks more than both of you know."

Ben had been sitting in Hugo's basement for five minutes before he realized what was wrong. It wasn't strange for Hugo to make small talk in monosyllables. It wasn't even strange for Hugo to look peaceful once in a while.

What was strange, even aside from the faint glowing of Hugo's skin in the dimness of the room, was the continued quiet.

The big stereo was off, the phonograph was silent, not even a transistor radio bleeped a sound.

"How come no noise?" Ben asked.

"Don't feel like it," answered Hugo, swallowing from a can of Coke. He scratched himself. Nothing new about the way Hugo scratched. He didn't shower too often, never had.

"Why don't you feel like it?" said Ben, pushing a little.

Hugo lifted his nearly colorless eyes to look at Ben. "The noise filled me up a lot of times when I was feeling empty," said Hugo. "I never feel empty any more. Don't know if you been there or not, since you haven't come in the motorboat with us, but get Anne to take you where she took me. You'll understand what I mean. I can't explain it in words that make any sense. Except to tell you that you're wanted, too."

So far, Ben hadn't learned anything new, but as the others were his only source of information about the light, he had to keep the conversation going.

Ben leaned forward. "I've been there. It's the island with the pool I used to sail to all the time. I was the one who brought Anne. Only the difference is—the thing scared hell out of me. Why aren't you afraid?"

Hugo glanced at the bright patch on the inside of his wrist. "I don't know. I have this great feeling of be-longing."

Just what Anne had said! Ben was excited. "Hugo —belonging? Belonging to what?"

Hugo's head swayed hypnotically. "I can't describe it exactly. Just I feel I belong, that I'm not alone, the way you and I used to talk about everybody in the long run being alone. I feel it less now, and not at all in the pool. No one's ever paid much attention to me except you, Ben. I'm not complaining. It's just the way it's been." Hugo took breath. "When I saw—felt—the light, none of that mattered any more. Something wanted me, asked for me. And I had to say yes. Yes. Take me. And Ben, I've felt—okay—ever since. There's really something inside me now, instead of that empty feeling. Even if I don't know why or what for." Hugo faltered. It was a long speech for him. "I can tell you don't approve, that I've given in to something I shouldn't, that I've given up. I even feel kind of like that myself, as if I've been taken over."

Hugo stood, paced the room, turned to face Ben.

"But I don't care. I don't care what you think or even what I think of myself. I only know that for the last few days, for the first time ever, something exciting has happened to Hugo van Paasen."

It seemed to come down to the same method each time, Ben realized. The light focused in on each one's source of pain and became the antidote.

But today, Hugo had added something new, given Ben a new thought. Hugo had used the phrase, "as if I've been taken over." A magnetic attraction, a seduction, a mental persuasion was one thing. External conquest by an external force. To be 'taken over' meant something more dangerous, more insidious. It suggested to Ben a kind of internal invasion, an internal alteration of the personality.

He supposed he was scowling, because when he said nothing, Hugo got uptight. "Don't holler at me—

you can't imagine how it feels, just once, not to be suicidally depressed."

Suicidally depressed? Since when was Hugo suicidally depressed! It reminded Ben of his conversation with David, of Anne's concentration on her foot. It seemed that the light not only located each one's source of discomfort, but amplified it to make it seem worse—in order to make it's antidote seem more attractive.

Ben answered Hugo quietly. "I wasn't going to holler. I just need to understand."

Ben saw Hugo's expression change. Suddenly he seemed crafty, aware.

"You mean you want to know what you're up against, don't you!" he demanded. "You're getting ready to fight whatever this is. I know you. I can tell. You can't stand surrender. You always need to fight, to be independent. Well, I don't. So don't fight for me, Ben. Whatever it means, whatever it is, *I want it!* I won't help you this time. I don't want to. I like what's happened to me, and I'll pay any price to keep it. So go away, Ben. We've been friends all our lives, but this time, count me out. And please—no speeches. I haven't the strength left to listen."

Ben made two more mental notes. The light not only increased perfectly normal sore points into agonies to make its own antidote seem more attractive, it also reduced, decreased, the strength to resist its power. Furthermore, the light made its subjects defend it, fight for it, fend off its enemies—in this case, Ben.

He crossed the room to touch Hugo's shoulder. "I understand. I could sure use your help with this. But I understand. So long, Hugo."

"So long, Ben."

He would see Lakey next.

Ben walked the mile out of Athens to the rundown farm, past the chicken coop and the pigpen to the shambles of aluminum sheeting and rough timber of the shack. Only this time, Lakey wasn't her normal, shapely bundle of flirtation. This time she was standing in front of a small mirror in the kitchen. When she turned at the noise of Ben's appearance, Ben couldn't believe what he saw. No longer the cheerful, oversexed Lakey; the girl who turned to face him, made up, blond hair piled high, wearing a tight, provocative dress, was asking—loud and clear and calm—for trouble.

"Good God, Lakey!" exploded Ben.

"I don't think God is good," said Lakey calmly. "If he were, he would care more. We're the poorest family in town. I haven't had a new dress or a decent pair of shoes since I can remember. But the light, Ben. The light is good. It makes sense."

"What kind of sense? What kind of sense?"

"The light says you should be comfortable, do what you want, get what you want," said Lakey, breaking away from him, using the old-fashioned sink pump to pour a glass of water.

And then Ben knew what kind of sense. The light, not of their earth, not human, had no human values. It simply gave each of them according to their need, different for Anne, for David and Janie, for Hugo, for Lakey. To Anne, release from being a cripple. To Hugo, release from loneliness. And for Lakey, comfort and possessions with a terrible twist: To use a natural, happy warmth to earn money without conscience or regrets, which the light had peacefully tranquillized inside her.

"But Lakey—think not just of now, but of the rest of your life," Ben said urgently, trying to get through.

"The rest of my life?" Lakey repeated in a blank tone. "It belongs to the light."

The implications of the light's power over human minds in terms of what Lakey was saying made one question more important than any other: What was the light going to do with those minds when it got them?

Lakey turned her attention back to her face and applied more eyeshadow to her already overdone eyes. She spoke excitedly, as if she were on a crazy high. "It can't hurt me. Nothing can hurt me now."

Ben left Lakey, feeling violently sick to his stomach.

On the way to see Jake, Ben passed David and Janie on High Street. Basically, they had been perfectly all right. So had most of the kids in town. It wasn't only the ones in trouble that the light had taken in. It was all of them. It just seemed that the changes were more visible in those who had had obvious problems.

Ben went through the Loring front gate. Mr. and Mrs. Loring were at work in their drugstore as usual. The house seemed empty. Ben found Jake in his room with Susan, both on a trip.

The small plastic bag of what looked like sugar, the hypodermic needle, the bent spoon, left no doubt as to what trip they were on. Nor did the small glass half-full of orange liquid. They were pretty high, both of them, giggling on the bed together, doing imitations of famous personalities. As Ben walked in, Jake was doing Johnny Carson interviewing Liza Minelli.

The light, of course. Destroying Jake and Susan by giving permission, by removing the guilt, making it easy for them to float away, never to be trapped in just Athens again.

As long as the light got them, Ben reflected, it simply didn't matter how.

He tried to calm his own panic at what was happening. And found himself racing—no way to talk to Jake or Susan in the space they were in—to find someone else, anyone else.

His friends, their younger brothers and sisters, even little ones, had altered. Some couldn't—or wouldn't—speak at all to him. And he could see a new calm, blank look on their faces. In the right lighting, the faint glow of their skins betrayed their submission, their collusion with the strange, unearthly force that, suddenly this summer, had entered their lives. More and more patches appeared on wrists, there was less and less real contact with him, even with one another.

"I know when one is dead, and one lives." The line from *King Lear* kept going through his mind.

All dead. None lives.

A frantic panic rose in Ben and nearly threatened his capacity to think or function at all. It was not a moment to dwell on possibilities, but to counteract the panic with direct action. What could he do?

Remembering the allegory of his childhood, he had a vivid memory of, after hours of watching the chickens, deciding it was time to track the fox.

He went quickly to the dock, set sail, and went to the part of the lake where he usually tacked toward the long island.

And that was all he managed. The winds were difficult, and when, good sailor that he was, he mastered the Pelican's maneuvers against the winds, there was a sudden storm. And when he fought the storm, his battle grew worse, less effective by the moment.

Until, quite simply, Ben knew he was barred from the island now. If the light could not force him to its will, it could prevent him from gathering the lab equipment, prevent him from confronting itself, prevent him from finding it out. The storm could even have been a coincidence. It was Ben's inability to conquer the weather that made the difference.

All right, he would wait. Endure, observe, try old methods, find new ones. He would be ready when an opportunity came to attack.

For the rest of July, Ben spent as many hours as he could sailing, an armload of books in the boat, alternately gliding across the water, swimming off the side of his boat, reading. He never got near the long island. He would head directly for the small cove where ordinarily he landed—and the wind would change, the boat veer away.

At sundown, after mooring his boat, Ben went home, ate, and began to roam, to track, to listen, to watch.

Anne's rented Starcraft never stopped until everyone under eighteen and over five or six had been taken to the light. All went one time, most more than once—according to Ben's tracking usually a minimum of three times each, as if it were a prescribed dosage.

After the boat trips, the older kids gathered together, banded around campfires in the mountains, near the river, anywhere for privacy. They formed circles with their arms about each other's shoulders and talked in hushed voices Ben couldn't hear without coming too close.

The reason they roamed and sailed freely by day, hid by night, was of course, the worsening condition of their skins. By now many of them glowed with an obvious phosphorescence in the complete darkness of night. Despite the warmth of summer, they wore long sleeves, brimmed hats to shield their faces. He supposed, if the light had a sense of humor, it might be amused at having created a new fad for winter clothes at the height of July. And it was all unnecessary. Neither he nor any of the adults could talk about it or do anything about it anyway.

The thought that the light might have a sense of humor rapidly opened a few more windows in Ben's mind. First, that the light was an entity, a personality with whom he was beginning to have a relationship as one living enemy has to his opposite, each psyching the other out, gathering knowledge of the other's strengths and weaknesses before the attack.

His second reaction to the possibility that the light might have a sense of humor—and therefore maybe a reachable intellect—was how young its humor was.

It could be just aping what it observed. But it took a capacity to think young to use patches, for instance. With its power to alter the entire nature of the skin, the only reason for patches on the inside of the wrist could very well be an imitation of their habit of using glow stamps for dances and parties. And the business with the clothes. And the weird music everyone was chanting lately during their gatherings. It sounded like songs they had heard on records, or on any rock radio station. Sounded like, but wasn't.

Because of the orb's terrifying power to influence, Ben had automatically concluded, probably based on too much science fiction, that it had to be old, to come from an older civilization. It had gotten here, hadn't it? Human beings couldn't do what the orb could do, could they? Conclusion: the experience of age. Maybe.

A young orb perhaps, from a more ancient experience than earth's. And if the orb were young, maybe there was a way Ben could relate to the orb's psychic processes.

Maybe. Everything was maybe.

But because he couldn't, wouldn't join, Ben was blocked by his friends as well as the light from coming too close to any explanation.

Often, in anger, Ben ricochetted back to the adults.

Most of them looked as blank as their children. They acted as if they were relieved at, rather than scared of, the changes, as if they were pleased at the new, un-expected sweetness, obedience to external rules that didn't matter anyway. No fists were swinging this sum-mer and everybody brushed their teeth. They all fol-lowed orders, outwardly. Nobody rebelled.

There were little things. Michael, for instance, whose hair had been longer than most football players wore it, cut it short at the merest suggestion. Janie, who had been stomping around defiantly wearing African turbans for a year, gave in to her parents' middle class tone-it-down-dear. And if Anne refused to have the operation, her parents seemed perfectly content that at least she was no longer behaving like a cripple. As for the Lorings, Ben suspected they would rather have Jake high than gone. What Lakey did at night was unmen-tionable now, but she and her stepfather and her small brothers had new clothes and new equipment for the farm.

There were just no hassles, and it was eerie.

Frustrated, Ben kept coming back to his mother and Mr. Osenko.

For the moment—though they looked far from blank—even their methods of communication seemed not to be working.

It was the most peaceful July in the history of Athens. Not a single juvenile arrest. Not a booking. Not even an unbanked fire on the beach.

At the beginning of August, two things happened.

6 : Banding Together

Ben was sharply aware of a new change in his friends. Their bodies twitched slightly, their hands shook, eyelids fluttered. They seemed to have less physical stamina, grew breathless from short walks, any physical effort. Except for trips across the lake and their evening meetings, mostly they just lay around. They seemed to be drained of something vital.

"Peaked," said Mrs. Donald. "They all look peaked. When you were little and you looked like that, I used to hang a piece of garlic around your neck. The German in your father used to laugh at my Roumanian habits. He said we believed too many of our own Dracula stories. Seemed to work, though," said his mother, adding pointedly, "kind of got the devil out of your system and put it at a distance."

"I probably got better just to get out of wearing the garlic," said Ben, but his mother's point was well taken. He remembered the old Dracula stories, the use of garlic, a smell vampires couldn't bear, to prevent them from sucking the blood of human beings.

A new development, Ben realized, nodding gratefully to his mother. The light, having drained their minds, was now draining their bodies.

Mr. Osenko, accepting a glass of cold lemonade, strained to speak to Ben. Again he could only quote to break the barrier of silence between them.

" 'The happiest youth, viewing his progress through, what perils past, what crosses to ensue, would shut the book, and sit him down to die,' " said Mr. Osenko. He also said, "Henry IV, Part Two, Act III, Scene i," as if he hoped Ben would remember the political disasters in England that made the king despair of the future of his country and wonder if the young would just give up and die.

Ben didn't remember much of the play, but he got Mr. Osenko's message. Disaster time.

All day, Ben renewed his frantic attempts to send messages, to speak to strangers passing through town, to telephone, to reread newspapers and listen to news reports, searching for clues to what might be happening in the outside world. No progress, and by evening he was nearly exhausted. Grimly, and without much hope, he then set out as usual for the island.

Maybe his alarm over the newest stage made him try harder, maybe the light was changing its tactics or growing less wary of Ben now that everyone else was conquered, but suddenly the second thing happened. Ben was allowed to land. That was the feeling. Allowed. Allowed to beach the boat, allowed to follow his customary path under the pine and birches toward the flat rock. There he felt a slight resistance, as if the light had become uncertain (as in the uncertainty of creatures his age from anywhere?), but he seemed able to push on. It became more difficult to move forward, and he remembered the early days of being magnetically pulled. The light's powers were extraordinary.

The last few yards, to get to the rocks at the edge of the pool, almost wore Ben out. But he made it.

The pool was there, then, his once quiet, deep pool of water, now changed and sinister. The luminescence had turned brilliant, the darting lights multiplied, the heaving of the water became violent.

As he stood at the pool's edge, he sensed a sudden invitation to—what?—view the triumph of the force beneath? Ridiculous, but Ben was near laughter again. He had to remind himself how horrible, how destructive the power of the light was, because for a moment he felt as if he were responding to an ego trip of someone his own age.

That was all right with Ben. Whether the light wanted to challenge him again at close quarters or was just showing off, Ben wanted to see again what he was up against. Stripping, he dove in, floated down in the dense oxygen, went through the moment of pain, entered the blackness.

He was not shocked, the change in the light was so logical. It had increased in size, its globe huge in the darkness, and its pulsations stronger. With each mind it conquered, each strength it drained, its power must enlarge correspondingly. It was like a conversion apparatus.

Converting us into what, thought Ben? Converting us into itself to become a single entity? More and more of one light? Or many lights? And was the process of conversion the final stage, or just the first stage of some as yet undefinable plan. Was there even a plan, an understanding of earth and its people—or did the light, happening here from somewhere, just have to wing it, so to speak.

And why only young people? More bendable, easier than trying to conquer adults, simply that they would live longer? Easier to feed with illusions, promises possibly. Or, and again the thought crossed Ben's mind, did the light itself have something in common with youth.

He had moved no nearer the orb, but his thinking began to grow slightly hazy as he tried to sort out his questions. The power was getting to him, of course.

Not me, Ben fought. Not ever.

He even made himself move closer to the white, breathing orb. Either he couldn't or the light wouldn't let him communicate directly, but Ben absorbed an exchange without words.

"You'll be mine, too," conveyed the light, pushing the thought through the density between them.

"You think so?" Ben pushed back. "I'll fight you every way I can, and if you can prevent me from getting outside help, I'll fight with whatever I've got inside me. And not just for myself, for the others, too."

If the white orb could laugh, Ben felt laughter. Young, like his own? Or laughter as old as the Universe. It came in waves across the thickened, more concentrated substance at the bottom of the pool, and then it stopped.

There was a deadly calm and in it a distinct threat.

The last thought Ben received was, "Remember the first book of your Bible? 'And God said, Let there be light' and then 'He made the stars also. And God set them in the firmament of the heavens to give light upon the earth, to rule. . . .' "

And with that bizarre use of the words from Genesis to justify its mission, the light instantly cut off transmission. The interview was ended.

Ben didn't know if he left the pool by his own will or was repulsed, but he was soon back in the middle of Crystal Lake, desperately trying to cope with every thought he had ever had on the subject of light: religious, philosophical, scientific. Because the orb had clearly established one factor: It had either known about the human mind before it got here or learned pretty quickly —enough in any case to be able to quote from its literature!

Forgetting to sail in his concentration on the orb,

Ben felt the Pelican broach to, swinging broadside to the waves. Rather than capsize, he decided to furl the sails and use the outboard motor. For a while, though, he remained motionless and leaned against the gun-whales to think.

Light, he prodded himself, associate every thought you can reach with the word "light."

Light meant revelation, knowledge, the ability to see, to understand.

Check: The orb knows more than we do, learns, understands more quickly than we do.

Light converts, conquers darkness.

Check: The light is converting, conquering us.

Light is a beacon, showing the way toward itself.

Check: The orb is leading us to the pool, into its own substance.

Light is pure energy.

Check: The orb is changing us into light. It wants more energy. For some reason, young human energy of mind and body.

Light travels faster than anything else in the Universe.

That thought had too many possibilities for Ben to come to any immediate conclusions. Being light, the orb was free to travel swiftly throughout the reaches of all space, possibly had been traveling for an eternity of time. Was it here now to stay? Would it move on again, taking the absorbed lives with it? Pure energy moved so quickly; think fast, Ben, think fast. Fast as light, fast as light, those words revolved in his brain, confusing his thinking until it occurred to him that he was still so physically close to the light that it could be creating a sort of static.

Ben gunned the motor and took off across the lake. Two other definitions of light came to Ben as his head cleared a little reaching the dock. Wanton, loose in morals. Also, frivolous, capricious, giddy.

A knowing, devouring, beckoning force with unknown moral character? No moral character? Ben sighed at the moon and shook his head. Only reflected light on a chunk of rock. But maybe there was a lesson in that. Resist like a rock, and he could bounce back the light of the orb. Of course light was also heat up close, and rocks could become molten lava and . . .

Shut up, Ben commanded his mind. Turn off any thinking process that drives you crazy and switch to gut reaction.

Check: Gut reaction is total terror. And when in total terror, if further action is impossible, get some sleep.

Anne was on the front porch when Ben got back to his house. Away from the moonlight, hidden in the shadows, covered entirely in the warm night by her clothing. As he saw her, he heard a rustling in the trees nearby. There were others with her. They banded together, never traveling alone anymore.

He wondered if he could touch her just once, the old way, the *normal* way. He took Anne's shoulders, bending to kiss her. He remembered other times, so many, before, when they had been close. This time, he knew even before he touched her nothing would happen, no feeling. And he was right. Her body stiffened, her lips were cool and still beneath his own, her feelings were far from him.

"Hi, stranger," he said, knowing he was a stranger now. All he could think of to add, like an idiot, was, "Want to go for a sail?"

Her laughter echoed weirdly. Her old bitter-funny tone returned for a moment. "I've got the Starcraft, remember, Ben? I don't need a run on the Pelican any more. Surely you've noticed—this summer?" And she laughed the weird laugh again.

"Yes," said Ben slowly, "I've noticed this summer." He wondered why Anne and the others were here.

"We've come to make it easier for you," said Anne, responding to his unspoken thought. "Hugo, Lakey, David—all of us want to try. We know how much you understand—and how little—about the light. But your questions will only be answered when you join us, when you become part of us. It's your holding back that's the trouble. For all of us. You'd know everything if you'd stop being so stubborn. And you know you're curious, Ben. . . ."

"Another form of seduction, tempting my curiosity?"

"Listen to what I'm saying." Anne's voice grew impatient. "We don't have to use words much any more."

"But I do? And you've been given permission to

communicate with me once more on my level?"

He must have sounded touchy, because Anne backed down. "I miss you, Ben," she said simply.

He longed to be close to Anne again, and for a moment she sounded nearly human. But he trusted nothing from her, the way she was now.

"Forget it," he said. And he left her and went into the house. He needed to be brief, to resist wanting her.

The long summer dogged on without much more change. At first he didn't think about it, but then he wondered—why no more changes? Could it possibly have something to do with him? Was that why Anne had come that day. Did the light need everyone?

When school began, there was a shift, a shift in feeling among the adults in Athens. Possibly the light had underestimated adult anger in human society at a lack of achievement in their young. It was one thing over the summer to watch their children laze around, but schooling was another matter.

The obedient, quiet children who, over the summer gave no trouble, now gave nothing at all.

If they didn't make too much noise in the halls, talk too much in class, steal occasionally, and occasionally smoke grass—neither did they work.

No one tried to compete on the sports field or in the gym or the swimming pool. No one competed for a decent mark, a good lab report, a decent enough poem for the school magazine, much less a decent grade.

They all simply sat in their classrooms, read when they were told to read, wrote what they were told to write. No questions. No originality. No active interest in their lives, in their futures, not even in what they were supposed to do the next day.

Zombies. In old Voodoo tradition, the dead made to walk again.

In Athens, the living made into the walking dead.

Frustrated, the adults could do nothing. But as if galvanized by their anger, Ben's own fury increased into more feverish attempts to get back to the island, to make some kind of assault on the light.

All the reading he had done that summer revolved in his head. He had read of theories that civilizations, which had gone beyond nuclear war, had developed mental abilities beyond those on Earth. Abilities to transform physical material into different shapes, into pure mental wave lengths, into anything, even pure energy. Able even to join themselves, their minds, together, so that many minds could form a single unit, a single force. He supposed that, no matter what Athens was going through, he had denied such possibilities with part of his mind, rejecting the whole business as if it were some kind of dream, some kind of fairy tale that would soon be over.

He was ready now to surrender all disbelief.

And he was going to get to the light if he died trying. And either deal with the light—or be destroyed by it. It was anger he felt, anger at being robbed of friends, of normal life, even of companionship at school that drove him now, not merely curiosity.

For some time every day, just as he had in the summer, Ben sailed toward the island. He tacked, fought winds, used a borrowed, more powerful outboard motor, struggled toward the point where he had once peacefully beached his boat. He tried different times of the day, in case the power of the light had peaks of strength and weakness. No time worked. The motor failed, the winds were too strong.

Then one evening, at dusk, as the sun set beyond the mountains and the last orange light played on the water of the lake, Ben saw a silhouette at the end of the dock where his boat was tied. He knew her shape in any light, in no light.

Why was Anne waiting for him, as clearly she was. The light's force? His own insistent anger?

When he came closer, she held out her hand—to indicate that they were still friends? To prevent him from assuming they were any more?

Like the rest, she was nearly translucent, so much thinner. If the adults had mentioned their appearance at all, it was merely to comment, as his mother had, that they seemed peaked. Nothing about the quality of their skins, their eyes enormous in their faces. Didn't they see —the adults—or didn't they want to see?

Anne came forward a little. She didn't speak, only motioned him toward the boat. He helped her in, careful of her foot, eager for what was to happen. He understood that if his anger was forcing the issue, it was the light who offered Anne as his escort, his passport.

He knew the wind would be perfect, the trip easy. It was. They beached on the island without effort, swiftly. For the first time in weeks, Ben followed the accustomed path under the trees, past the flat rock, to the edge of the pool.

Anne withdrew into the shadow of the trees. She hadn't said a word throughout the crossing, and neither had Ben. He was to be allowed to visit the light. For the moment it was all that mattered. But he couldn't help but wonder why. Was he right in thinking that for some reason the light had to have him, too?

The pool gleamed eerily, turbulent, the darting lights were more numerous.

Ben sensed greater power, but his own fury, he decided, was more than equal to whatever lay below.

He dove in quickly, past the pain, touching all nerves, and down to the bottom, the darkness.

At the end of the darkness, there was the light.

Ben was terrified at what he saw. The original pulsing orb had grown to an unfathomable size, as large as the sun seemed to be. And the orb didn't just pulse. It pounded, expanded and contracted with an incredible power. It seemed to contain enough strength to explode half the world.

If just in Athens there were enough young minds to increase its size to this extent, what could happen if it devoured even more of humanity?

Without knowing or even stopping to think whether

he could actually communicate with the light, Ben blurted out, "How many minds are you after? What will you take in exchange for the lives of my friends? Are there more of you in other parts of my country, of this planet? What do you want of us? What do you need us for? Is there anything in me you will take in exchange for my friends?" He could hear his own language growing stilted and slow, the way one might speak to an alien.

Silence followed Ben's outburst. Absolute silence.

He knew the minute his words were out, the light would ask for the one thing Ben couldn't give. In the silence, Ben could feel the light pull at his mind, stronger than before. All he could hang onto was knowing that the fate of the young people in Athens, his own fate, depended on his resistance to the seductive, horrible force.

The light didn't answer. It just pulled harder.

Ben wouldn't give in. He couldn't think clearly, but it did seem that the victims had to be willing, and he wasn't, no matter what the light promised. Even Anne, all his friends around him again. It wasn't enough.

Except for the light's show of power, of size, it seemed to be stalemate again between Ben and the light.

Then just before Ben was permitted to withdraw, he was sent reeling backward with a sudden onslaught of vibrations, and he saw the light pounding like a giant pulse. He was being threatened with something, and he knew it. The light was angry, too.

Its unspoken message was clear. Ben, or Ben through someone else, was to be punished. When the message was received, the pounding of the orb subsided slightly. There was nothing further, and Ben was released.

He surfaced to find Anne waiting for him at the pool's edge, her face full of questions she never asked.

Using all his strength, the fullest of his own mental power, Ben managed one thing before he followed Anne back across the island to the boat.

He grabbed one jar from the equipment he had left behind the trees.

Anne slipped silently away from him when they docked. And for the moment, that was perfectly all right with Ben. The only thing he wanted was to get to the lab at school as fast as possible.

He let himself into the school easily through a half-open basement window. Doors were rarely locked in the high school. The third-floor chemistry lab was open. He hadn't been good at chemistry last year. He desperately needed Hugo's help, except he knew Hugo wouldn't—or couldn't give it.

Ben put the jar full of the gaseous matter on the first table. He lit a burner and gathered the apparatus he thought he would need, an Erlenmeyer flask, a fifty-milliliter gas measuring tube, stirring rods, an evaporating dish, test tubes, a hundred milliliter beaker. He trapped a quantity of the gas in the jar into a syringe and began to work.

When he had done several experiments with the gas, he made slides, particularly of the matter that contained the darting lights.

He worked all night, not daring to stop. But unless he had missed something, he came up with nothing at all. The gas was the usual composite of elements air normally contains—nitrogen, oxygen, the rest—there was only the faintest trace of something he could not define, not much, not enough to make such a difference. All he found on the slide of the bright material was phosphorous.

How did such ordinary stuff make such extraordinary differences in gaseous matter? How significant could such a small trace of an unfamiliar element be? Was it even unfamiliar? Or had Ben forgotten his chemistry? He needed Hugo. Only Hugo no longer needed him.

As Ben felt his way through the darkened hallways of the school, he tripped across two bodies who shrank away from his presence.

Jake and Susan rose, startled and unsteady, to their feet.

"Are you all right?" said Ben. "Tell me."

They raced from him, at first fading into the shadowy corridor, and then stopping at the far end. As if in a gesture of farewell, they lifted their concealing hats.

And Ben knew the orb's punishment. Jake's and Susan's skins were no longer merely phosphorous. He could see right through them. They had been energized into pure light. But since they retained the suggestion of their forms and features, Ben could see something even more grotesque.

They were smiling.

7 : Changes

The following day, Jake and Susan were missing.

Ben realized the light's logic in picking those two first. The town would simply expect that they had finally run away as they had always threatened to do.

After several days of the usual turmoil over teen-age runaways, neither police nor parents could find a trace of them.

"Are you sure they didn't say anything?" Mrs. Loring kept asking every one of them as they went in and out of the drugstore. "I mean, one of them might have let something slip about where they were going. Are you sure, any of you?"

Her distress was painful only to other adults and to Ben. On the faces of those whom the light had touched were fleeting secret smiles as they nodded to each other.

Ben caught up with Anne as she left the drugstore.

"You act as if you knew this would happen," said

Ben grimly. "Did you know? Were you warned?"

"We knew," said Anne.

"Why do you all act as if you were fated for some sort of marvelous destiny?"

"We are," said Anne.

"Will you stop being so damned—serene—about people just fading out of sight," said Ben. "And I wish I could stop thinking of that Pied Piper poem we learned as kids."

They walked for a while. Anne bent to pick a wild flower from the undergrowth at the edge of the road. When she stood, Ben saw a saddened expression on the unnatural glow of her face.

"I think of that poem, too," she said. "Do you remember it pretty well? All those lovely things the Pied Piper promised?

'Where waters gushed and fruit-trees grew,
And flowers put forth a fairer hue,
And everything was strange and new. . . .'
"And the part about:
'When lo, as they reached the mountain-side,
A wondrous portal opened wide,
As if a cavern was suddenly hollowed;
And the Piper advanced and the children followed,
And when all were in to the very last,
The door in the mountain-side shut fast.
Did I say all? No! One was lame,
And could not dance the whole of the way. . . .'"

Anne gathered more flowers, black-eyed susans and Queen Anne's lace, and held them against the long sleeves of her shirt.

"The lame boy talked about it the rest of his life," she finished. "Remember?"

She went on with the poem.

> " *'And just as I became assured*
> *My lame foot would be speedily cured,*
> *The music stopped and I stood still*
> *And found myself outside the hill,*
> *Left alone against my will,*
> *To go now limping as before,*
> *And never hear of that country more!'* "

She was breaking Ben's heart. He had thought the light had helped Anne to forget she was crippled. Certainly she used the brace less and less. But all this time she was frightened that after all she might be left out of the final—what should he call it—the final promise of peace, death-life, whatever it was, and would be left behind because of her foot. And yet she went on doing the Pied Piper's work, leading the others to what she might never have for herself.

"I'll give you, you've got guts," said Ben. "I may not agree with anything you're doing, Anne, but I'll give you, you've got guts."

She laughed the first normal laugh he'd heard in a long time.

"A romantic turn of phrase if there ever was one," she said in the old flirting way. "You always did know how to sweet-talk a girl."

The small, light moment was over. They heard the rustling of the band of others, following her, in the trees nearby. She left him to go to them, and he was again alone.

As he turned, Ben could hear the singing begin. Hugo had begun to hold masses for strange gods, on the dock sometimes, in the woods between the Athens houses and the school, on the cliff of Bear Mountain. The chanting of the self-abasing masses made Ben's blood run cold. Not the nonsensical content of the praying, but the kids collected together behaving like a mindless entity.

Pieces of their protests from the summer came back to him.

"Don't save me," Hugo had said. "I'm not alone any more. People listen to me now, they accept me. I'm part of something."

And Jimmy, hostile at Ben's interference. "Cut it out. You don't know what it's like to be pushed into something you don't really want all the time—just because your parents think its great. The light accepts you as you are, everyone becomes the same."

"You want to be the *same?*" Ben had asked. Being part of other people he believed in. Being the same made him shudder. He had been brought up on differences, on the uniqueness of each.

Jake and Susan and Lakey he could almost understand. They had never been as strong and special as some of the others: Hugo, Jimmy, David, Janie. But weak or strong, special, ordinary—the light seemed to make no distinction.

All of them said the same things. "Stay away. Leave us alone. Don't protect us or fight for us. We want to be together in the light."

None of them interpreted what was happening as being controlled.

"Not controlled, Ben," said Anne. "Given."

No one. No one cared but him.

Why should he bother if no one cared? This could be going on all over the world for all he knew. How many were fighting? How many were giving in? And why did the light seem to want him, too, when it had all the others? He still couldn't get a word out and nothing even faintly recognizable as trouble got in. More times than he wanted to consider, he felt like something out of a ridiculous science fiction plot. He could see a future headline: BOY LOCKED UP FOR FANTASIZING OUTER SPACE TAKEOVER AND BELIEF IN SAME.

Ben caught himself up immediately. Wallowing in self-pity, are we?

Solitude was a sure cure. He collected his sleeping bag and camping gear and stormed up Bear Mountain to stay for a whole weekend.

He came down sober.

And he came down looking for Mr. Osenko.

Ben had ended his contemplation on the mountain by hearing his father's voice. "When looking for treasure, if you don't find it in the first hole you dig, you dig another. When looking for answers, if you don't find them by digging through the same old patterns of thought, dig for new ones in different places in yourself. And if that doesn't work, go to someone else. But don't talk. Shut your mouth, open your mind, and listen!"

Mr. Osenko was in the vegetable garden.

"Please talk to me," said Ben. "I understand the paralysis, but try, if you can."

Mr. Osenko plucked calmly at weeds. For him to speak, Ben knew, was a strain, but unlike most of the adults he didn't seem intimidated by the power that was consuming them.

"Mencius, the great disciple of Confucius, said, 'A *ming-t'ang* is the abode of a real king. If Your Majesty wishes to put into effect the rule of such a king, do not tear it down.' "

"Terrific," said Ben wrily. "Now how do I figure that one out?"

Mr. Osenko smiled and opened his hands in a gesture of "you know that's all I can do." Then he stuck his hands in his pockets and moved toward the small meadow behind the Donald house. Tall weeds, wild flowers, and farther on near the brook, willows grew.

Ben followed him, scowling over his attempt to interpret Mr. Osenko's quote. What was the message? Preserve the power of the light, only take it for himself? Was Ben then to take over rather than destroy the power of the light? And if Ben were to conquer the power of the light, what was he to do with it? Power was not something Ben wanted. He must have misunderstood.

At the edge of the narrow brook, Mr. Osenko paused and fed another quote into Ben's mental digestive system. Another quote from *King Lear,* because he knew Ben was familiar with the play, this one from Act III, scene iv.

" 'Why, thou wert better in thy grave than to answer with thy uncovered body this extremity of the skies.' "

Chinese. English. It wasn't important where the quotations came from except that they seemed contradictory to Ben. On the one hand, Mr. Osenko advised a takeover, but without tearing down the *ming-t'ang,* the existing structure, meaning the light. On the other hand, he was warning Ben against the powers of the universe.

Ben struggled to sift Mr. Osenko's words.

"Don't analyze," cautioned Mr. Osenko. "Keep it simple. Sift knowledge intuitively." With which, he ambled back across the meadow.

Simple! Okay, simple.

A takeover without destruction made sense. He knew without question no physical force, no chemicals, nothing material could destroy the light anyway. It had to be an intellectual, a psychic, an emotional combatant of some kind.

But what inside him could he use to fight without endangering himself in the presence of this apparition, presumably from the skies? The light had to be seduced into combat in a way that would amuse it, give it pleasure, throw it off its guard to begin with, as if it were a game. A game it felt it could win maybe, to give it a comfortable feeling of superiority.

Think back to what there is in me that keeps me from being drawn in, reflected Ben. Think about me.

Keep it simple, Mr. Osenko had said.

I care about others, but I care about myself first. If I'm not all right, I'm no good to anybody was something Ben had learned from his mother.

I need people, but separately from myself. I want to love and be loved by others, but not to become one with another. I don't like to blur and blend my own sense of identity. These were things Ben had learned for himself in relating to other people.

I need to be part of other lives, but never to surrender my own. Surrendering to anything other than what feels comfortable to me, what I feel I can live with, is impossible.

Reduce meditation to its bottom line, his father had said, a simple, clear thought.

I am me, was the simple thought, and I defy anything that wants to absorb me into a collective "we."

I will not be destroyed, eaten alive, was the next thought.

Self-preservation is the basis of sanity, without

which I can save nobody, came next.

The bottom line then reduced itself to a single word: Self.

Ben felt like an idiot. Why had it taken him so long to figure out that it was simply his own clinging to himself as an important matter that had defied the light's power? And maybe that was why the light seemed to want him so much. Because he valued himself, the light did, too.

All right then. The issue was the single mind against the collective.

Now about the game, a deadly game that required weapons. He needed tools that were not destructive in the usual way but would destroy the power of the light.

As if on cue, Mr. Osenko reappeared. Ben watched as he emerged from the house to wander the far end of the meadow. The old man didn't come near Ben, but he waved a friendly greeting with a hand that held a familiar object. It was a battered old volume of Voltaire, the French philosopher whose ideas about liberty and equality had stirred up a lot of revolutions.

The friendly gesture with the book gave Ben an idea, an idea he thought Mr. Osenko was trying to convey.

In seconds, the idea grew into a plan.

8 : The Light

There were three things Ben was certain of now.

The first was that they were right—the scientists involved in raising more government money for SETI, the Search for Extraterrestrial Intelligence—on the assumption that our biological evolution on Earth was not a unique miracle, but was likely to have occurred on other similar planets in the cosmos. In Athens, not only had an extraterrestrial creature proved it existed, it had arrived to say hello in person, exuding at least one quite human characteristic, the need to dominate.

How Ben wished he could write to the people at SETI and resolve once and for all the controversy over the existence of extraterrestrial intelligence. That it not only existed but bore strikingly similar personality traits. Only any letter he wrote now would disappear.

So, yes, there was intelligent life elsewhere. It could look and behave differently, but—at least in this case—

it had enough of our own characteristics to make it understandable and therefore beatable.

And it had to be beatable, because Ben's second certainty was that soon there would be no life left untouched in Athens. Having paralyzed the adults into complete inaction, the light was repeating the process it had used on Jake and Susan almost daily. Why it had waited so long, he didn't know.

David, his younger sister, and Janie were next, almost as if the light were removing them in clusters of loyalty groups. Ben didn't see it happen this time, but it had to have been the same process that had taken Jake and Susan. The final transformation into pure light, pure energy, and the disappearance of their physical forms on Earth.

Whether the light simply absorbed them or transmitted them to some other civilization, Ben couldn't yet know. Nor did he understand the light's sequence of choices. All that mattered now was to reverse the light's processes.

His third certainty was that Mr. Osenko had helped him arrive at the only workable weapon possible to an Earth-human mind: the self and the vision of self that the greatest minds had projected. What would happen he didn't know. Whether he could actually defeat the light simply with "ideas" he couldn't be sure. There was no point in dwelling on the abstract outcome of a duelling game when you've only got one choice of weapons.

For the few days after his conversation with Mr.

Osenko, Ben collected his weapons. He hated taking so much time when his friends were disappearing, but he didn't dare rush at the light without being prepared.

As if Mr. Osenko's strength against the power of the light were growing, too, with his effort to collaborate with Ben, he checked on what Ben was doing and nodded his approval.

Ben's weapons were, of course, books. His selections were careful, but he wished now that he had read more widely, had some of Anne's background. He began with his favorite history book, *The Rise of the West*. He added a book on the history of Eastern civilization, another by Robert Leakey on the early struggles of human beings down from the trees. But not only books of history, anthropology, science, poetry. Ben added his mother's guitar, a collection of art reproductions, and, to feed the light's possible youth and certain sense of humor, he threw in a deck of cards.

His collection was intended to carry out his plan: the battle of the independent struggling "I" against the collective "We." It was an assortment of Earth's wisdom and fun, the strength that came from progress and search, against what he hoped was the stagnant complacency of an identity that had so far stopped growing itself that it had to absorb energy from other beings. If he could make the orb realize its own deficiencies, he hoped the shock would send it reeling out of his life and the lives of everyone in Athens.

When Ben was ready, he went into the kitchen to

explain to his mother what could be an absence for several days, a week, however long it took. To tell her somehow what he was doing, what he was up against, the possibility even that he might lose, might not come back at all.

She had seen the packed duffles of course.

And she spoke before he even opened his mouth. Mopping the endlessly busy sink with her pink sponge, she poured them each a cup of coffee and plumped herself calmly onto a kitchen chair.

"You can't tell me and for some reason I know why you can't," she said, debating over a third spoonful of sugar and deciding she needed the comfort. "It's just come time to do something about that fox, I suppose."

That his mother could say such a thing must mean that, like Mr. Osenko, she had gathered some strength of her own in her complicity with Ben against the light.

He acknowledged the courage behind her acceptance that there wasn't any other way. "This time, I'm a little better armed, I hope," said Ben.

"Well, you never were bent on killing things," answered his mother. "You scared the one fox away with just your water pistol. Worked, didn't it?"

"It did work, didn't it," said Ben, grateful for the memory and its message. If his mother wasn't going to wallow in negative possibilities, neither was he. And if it came to that, he didn't have to win by killing either. He only had to chase away, or maybe in this case, unplug the power.

So as Ben got up to go, "Good luck," was all his mother said, and all Ben answered was, "Don't worry if I'm late, ma."

The Pelican was in good shape. He had seen to that. Wind or no wind, permission or not, he was going to get to the island.

The wind was against him.

Ben figured that.

The outboard motor was out of commission. The light had arranged for one of the kids, obviously, to make sure of that, too.

Only this time, Ben was prepared to do battle on the simplest possible level—human endeavor. The single-minded purpose of a single human being. Nothing psychic could fight him today, not against the simple, primitive method of using a paddle, with the simple, primitive will of a human being behind it.

For an afternoon and half the night, Ben paddled.

It was two in the morning when he made it to the island, with the sensation that his theory was working. Pushed by fear, anger, and self-preservation, the individual "I" could begin to tackle the tyranny of a "we."

He carried his duffles of books and games and the guitar across the island. It was not easy, but it was not as difficult as he had thought it might be. Either the orb was tired, or it was growing curious over his persistance.

Without pausing, he dove with all of his gear into the pool.

The light—huge, pulsing—gave off distinctly angry

vibrations, uneven, as if it were trying to warn him, stop him with a sort of cosmic temper tantrum.

Ben wasn't allowed close, but at a distance, apparently, the light couldn't stop him altogether, couldn't dismiss him.

Ben sat, crosslegged, facing the huge, glittering orb.

He began, planning to talk first, then read by the orb's own light.

"I don't know exactly where you come from. But I sure as hell know what you want." The light seemed quieter for a moment, as if it were listening. "And there's no way you're going to use up any more kids in this town as energy fodder or mind fodder or whatever you're using them for. Since you're plugged into my head, you know the stuff I've been thinking. I mean, I don't know if there's one of you in Athens or a lot of you all over the Earth. I don't know where you come from or what you're going to do with us, whether you come from a strong civilization wanting to conquer us or a dying civilization that simply wants to live here.

"I suppose you must come from a more advanced scientific culture than us because you've been able to figure out how to get loose from your system and survive. Only even if your civilization is older, there's something about you that makes me think you're about my age. And if I'm right, you might be interested in a little game I want to play. I challenge you to listen to what I have to say, to do what I want you to do, *or* to come up with something better.

The light's initial response was an instant puffing up, a sudden surge of power. From some other source? Or had it drawn more energy from town. Hugo. Or Lakey. Anne?

Get going, Ben prodded his head, dumping out the contents of the duffles.

"Ready?" said Ben. "The game is to pit about a million and a half years of our fighting to be unique, each of us part of but different from the other, against your sort of blob conformity. People on earth may share certain basic elements, emotions, genetic traits, but each combination is different, and we like it that way." He knew his tone of voice was weird, half-lecture, half-talk, but he didn't know how else to get the serious part of the game across, to say nothing of how you talk to someone who doesn't talk back. Uncomfortably he went on. "We're pretty independent here, and I don't think you're going to find it too easy to turn us into one large, computerized lump. Besides I'd like to see what you have to offer, besides mindless peace."

The light had stopped puffing up, but it seemed to settle, to hold its pulsation pattern without change. At least it had stopped growing for the moment.

He had to attack, go on with the game. He held the fat history of Western civilization in his hand. "Our human ancestors had to be strong, independent types to have the courage and the sense to leave the trees, descend to the plains of Africa in search of food. Strong, independent minds formed the Earth's early civilizations and each added to our growth and knowledge." He was pleased with the notes he had made and memorized, so he wouldn't get confused under fire. He went on with the lecture.

"The Egyptians were great on mathematics and astronomy, the Israelites formulated the ethical and moral basis of Western civilization. It was the Greeks who first understood the concept of ideas, the Chinese minds whose emphasis on mental and emotional balance, to say nothing of their discovery of gunpowder, influenced more than half the world. And not only did each civilization contribute its unique characteristics to our history, but so did unique minds."

Ben drew breath and plunged ahead, drawing on whatever names came into his head.

"There were the great artists of the Renaissance, Leonardo da Vinci, Michelangelo. There were writers like Shakespeare, Dostoyevsky, Flaubert, Lady Murasaki, Dickens. Scientific minds: Galileo, Freud, Einstein. Political minds from Plato to Jefferson to Karl Marx. And our musical minds: Bach, Mozart, the Beatles, Simon and Garfunckel." Ben knew the last two groups didn't exactly match, but he liked them and they had a youth quality he thought might interest the light. "Anyway," finished Ben for the moment, "what makes you think you can change our heritage of independent thought, the products of individual great minds, and substitute some kind of collective mediocrity?" The last part was a phrase he had heard and liked, and again he waited for a response.

Nothing. Why wasn't the light playing, picking up the gauntlet, fighting back? He paused for a few more seconds, waiting for some reaction. He had thought maybe vibrations of laughter, scorn at the beginning—something.

And then he did see something. There was a slight reaction in the light, just slight. But it was the sign Ben had hoped for. He *had* found the right weapon, even if he was still using it clumsily. The reaction he saw was the merest slowing of the regular throbbings of the light.

No wonder the light seemed to have lost its sense of humor.

Ben was getting through!

"Okay!" said Ben. "Maybe now it's my turn to have some fun." He grimaced mockingly at the light. "I'm just going to sit here," he said, "and read to you, play music for you, show you paintings—even amuse you with board games and magic tricks with cards—until one of us gives in."

There was a vibration then. Ben seemed to read it as a come-on.

"Fine. But I can promise you, it won't be me who collapses. You didn't want me to come today, but I got here, and maybe you still want me and you still think you can get me. Maybe for some reason this time you haven't the power to make me leave. I don't understand exactly what I'm doing yet, but I promise you—I *will!*"

Ben began to read. He started with passages from Leakey's *Origins,* describing the brain power, the daring of early manlike creatures, slower, weaker than all other animals, to become rulers of their world, human beings. He read from the Bible, the story of a man who led an enslaved people across deserts to their own land, Israel, a people who fought for their political but mostly spiritual survival. He read about Christ, whose teachings added the concept of love to justice. He read from Plato and Aristotle, concepts of the human condition. He read from Freud, the workings of the human psyche. He read from Einstein and Hoyle, concepts of science and the universe. He held up to the light paintings by Leonardo and Rembrandt and Van Gogh. And he used the guitar to do what he could with music, from Gregorian chants to Jethro Tull.

Hour after hour Ben went on, alternately reading, showing, playing music, all the monumental contributions of Earth's people. He didn't leave out the Hitlers, the Spanish Inquisition, the rape of China, or the physical diseases, the crimes, the wars, murders, prejudice, pollutions—but always, he hammered, people on Earth fought back, for liberty, justice, sanity, health, against whatever odds.

"And we'll bloody well fight you, too," Ben finished, "whoever and whatever you are."

He had been playing a Simon and Garfunkel song with the line "I am a rock" in it. When he put the guitar down, he looked up for the first time in nearly twelve hours. He had purposely avoided checking the light in order to concentrate, and, just in case, in order not to be discouraged.

When he faced the light, he felt first shock, and then elation.

Without a sound or further vibration, the orb of light had shrunk almost in half. Its throbbing had decreased to a vague, erratic beat.

Whatever Ben had done had been the right thing. The deadly game had worked. The power of the light had weakened. Now he could begin to believe that the job could be accomplished.

Sitting there at the bottom of the pool with a lot of faith, however, wasn't enough. Action was still required. What had worked best? The reading? The music? The story of humanity's struggle toward individuality and independence?

Ben desperately needed sleep. But if what he was doing was killing the power of the light, he would go on until he dropped.

He began again from the beginning.

He had started on Friday. By Monday morning, he could go on no longer. He'd been at it for three and a half days, no sleep, no food.

He didn't dare leave, fearing the light would recover its strength. Rejuvenate itself by drawing energy out of his friends. By absorbing them. Or, as Ben had come to believe, using their minds for some unknown purpose.

As Ben went on with the game, he had a vision of the transformation of Jake and Susan into outlines of pure light, luminescent outlines of what had once been physical forms. The light, which had begun by draining the strength of their minds and bodies, had now learned a way to absorb them completely. The vision of what had happened to Jake and Susan was accompanied by a strong image of the orb as a kind of vast, computerized mind system, and if that were true, was it possible that the initial purpose of the orb was to LEARN?

It was so logical! An alien thing arrives with a limited knowledge of a system's inhabitants. Since it clearly plans to do something about the inhabitants, it must first understand them. So not only does it discover it can use our energy to make itself stronger, it finds a way to absorb us in order to take us into itself and learn how we function, what we think, and put every brain cell, every bone tissue, every muscle, organ, and body system under it own form of microscope.

Two frighteningly important things weren't clear.

The purpose of the orb's need to learn.

And whether it was alone.

If it could command some kind of reinforcement— a parent system? similar entities?—the orb would be harder to beat.

A few hours later, Ben had had it. He couldn't go on without sleep or food any longer.

Would there be a change, a strengthening in some of his friends with the light weakened now? A sort of reverse process? Could he find someone to take over for him? Anne maybe? Or Hugo? Could he force the light to let go of anyone? To halt the mind-collecting, the body absorption?

Ben struggled against sleep as long as he could. He shook his intellectual fist until the moment came when he knew he was finished.

His only relief as he knew he was about to pass out was also knowing he had found, if not the secret to its final defeat, at least a way to control, diminish, the orb's power. The self against the mind-group could win. Why, he didn't know for sure. Except maybe that the individual cared what happened, and perhaps the group didn't.

But he needed help. There was no way to do this alone. Especially if the orb could somehow holler for reinforcement.

As Ben grew weaker with the need for sleep, he felt the orb grow a little more again.

He forced himself awake.

Only how long could he last? He was too tired even to use anger as adrenalin.

And then, in his last waking second, a terrible sound reached him, and a broad streak of dark, red light.

9 : The Red Streak

The red streak of light bulleted through the density of the pool to pierce the orb.

"Guess that answers one of my questions," Ben said grimly to himself, feeling half-mad talking to himself aloud, but then, "Why not?" he said. "They can read me anyway. So the light is able to signal for help and get it. And get it. And get it," he repeated, as the red streak continued to pour its torrent of energy into the orb.

And he saw, with the infusion of the red streak, the orb grew stronger again, not as large as before, but pulsing more steadily. It was as if not only strength but some kind of communication had been sought for and found, a renewed confidence.

All right, but he'd found something, too. The orb's weakness, the way to defeat it. The light might be able to draw on strength beyond itself, strength to give it strength, but not enough to grow back to its original size. So Ben's general method, his game plan, was correct.

If he could just keep at it.

And then he heard, or absorbed, two distinctly impossible words.

"Oh, yeah?"

The words were followed by an equally incredible visual phenomenon.

For a brief moment, the rim of the gleaming circle altered, dissolved, and became a form. And then not one but many forms, altering, dissolving, gleaming softly as they melted together and separated out, melted and separated again as if they could choose many shapes to be, and then at last chose. Chose the distinct shape and laughing features of young males and females about his own age, and one male, larger, more aggressive than the rest, came a little forward, confident and sure. Cocky was more like it. And there was nothing otherworldly about the laughter either. It was more like the kind of hoot Ben associated with the locker room at school after their basketball team had won another game.

"This can't be happening," Ben blurted out. Really clever, that remark!

"Says who," responded his opposite from across the pool, folding healthy, athletic arms across its chest.

Also a clever remark! A possible first conversation anyone on Earth had had with anyone from out *there*, and listen to them both! Well, what would history expect at first sight, the Gettysburg Address?

Funny contrast, though, to the heavy exchanges of their minds.

Funny! There is nothing remotely funny about this, thought Ben.

"Sure there is," said his opponent, as the others milling behind him laughed again, the arrogant, over-bearing sound of a winning team. "What's funny is how we're going to win. Hands down. Wanna bet? I'll even give you odds."

Poor Anne, thought Ben, with her Robert Browning poetry. And all the people who dreamed rapturously of the mysteries of outer space to electronic music. This guy sounds like he's running a cosmic horse race! Like an idiot.

"Who's the idiot," came the answer, soft and threat-ening again.

And the voices swarming behind him echoed the same soft threat, as the figure of the boy and his com-panions dissolved once more into Ben's familiar enemy, the pulsing and deadly orb.

Another set of speculations were satisfied. The orb was a collective mind, many minds, separate beings when they chose, but all one, all the same, all with connected thought patterns and responses, responding to a lead mind, a primary leader. Yes, the light had a personality, many in one. Yes, it could command help, probably others like itself still out there somewhere, acting as rear guard as one or more orbs made a descent into an alien atmosphere. Yes, it was as young, they were as young as he had supposed, as well as armed with the tools, the knowledge of an older, more sophisticated culture. Minds from where? A disintegrated system maybe from which they had had to learn to break free or be destroyed, floating through millions of space miles to find another home? It seemed logical. And absolutely terrifying.

And, yes, Ben was the idiot. Trapped, soothed, delayed momentarily by the fun of talking to his counterpart.

GET OUT OF HERE!

Get food, sleep, help, something. But get out, Ben commanded his exhausted being.

Too tired to endure it, Ben lost consciousness at the level of pain as obviously the light meant him to in its effort now to keep him down. But even subconsciously his resistance must have worked, because when he woke, he was at the pool's edge. Collapsed, but at least on the surface of the world again.

He remembered first the brilliant red streak as the most dangerous of the phenomena he'd seen, a force from only the Universe knew where that had helped the orb pulse more strongly against him again. Were there other strengths it had brought to the light? Was there now something more to deal with?

No matter. What he had been doing all weekend had worked. He had found at least the beginning of the way.

If only for moral support, Ben's every instinct was to find Mr. Osenko. He got himself back across the long island and unbeached the Pelican. Just being on Earth where he belonged freshened his spirit. The day was clear, the autumn air sparkled on the lake, the boat moved swiftly with the wind. He reveled in it all.

Ben docked at Athens' wharf and went immediately home.

"Ben, eat something," said Mrs. Donald, horrified at the sight of him, wild-eyed with exhaustion and whatever else.

"I need Mr. Osenko," Ben answered.

"In the vegetable garden, I think," she said, fortunately understanding that one need can sometimes supercede all others.

Ben went out the back door.

Mr. Osenko was on his knees, planting parsley, something that would grow in the colder weather of autumn. Good to see something normal, simple, earthy, like Mr. Osenko planting seeds, his hands poking and patting soil.

As Ben came upon him, kneeling in the vegetables, Mr. Osenko looked up. He blinked in the early morning sunlight, took thought, and said, " 'Ask, and it will be given you; seek and you will find. . . .' "

"Yes," said Ben promptly, relieved that their technique of communication still worked. "I hope you can help, Mr. Osenko, because after what I've just been through, I can sure use it." Ben couldn't, of course, speak openly of the light, of the many minds in the light, but he could hope. And project as hard as possible the insanity around them. "Please understand whatever you can, say whatever you can. Help me. I've begun, but it's not enough."

Mr. Osenko rose slowly from his knees, brushing soil from his trousers and his hands.

" 'We are such stuff as dreams are made on, and our little life is rounded with a sleep.' "

"No," said Ben, recognizing the lines from Shakespeare's *Tempest* and recognizing that Mr. Osenko was offering him an out if it all got to be too much, a possible thought that what happened didn't matter too much. "No," repeated Ben. "It all matters. Everything matters. The work we've done on this planet does matter, that we are conscious and trying matters." Ben grinned, even in fatigue. "This stage on this Earth in this system is our reality. And I won't let go, have it taken from us."

In the morning sun, Mr. Osenko smiled his approval. And suddenly spoke, under the circumstances, some lines almost indecently silly.

> *"Jack be nimble*
> *Jack be quick*
> *Jack jump over*
> *The candlestick."*

Ben remembered that Mr. Osenko, among his favorite Shakespeare plays, philosophers, and assorted poets, had also taught them nursery rhymes because he said they all had a history. What was this one? To jump over the candlestick, lighted, and extinguish the light, was good luck.

It was exactly what Ben had been doing. Trying, with himself as one form of Earth's endeavor, to jump over, extinguish the extraterrestrial light.

Mr. Osenko was encouraging him.

But Ben had tried all he knew—what else was there to do?

He entreated Mr. Osenko with every source of energy in his mind. And then, in a rush, there was a responding source of energy.

Ben had never needed it before, never been open to it before, never knew that Mr. Osenko possessed the ability to telepathize. Mental telepathy wasn't something he had either believed or disbelieved in until recently, and then only in connection with the light.

"Thank heaven you're desperate enough to receive from me now," telepathized Mr. Osenko. "I've been trying to get through for weeks. The light doesn't seem to be able to interrupt the electrical impulses of our brains nearly as well as it can shut off the physical use of our tongues. I've been trying to *will* you into receiving. But of course that doesn't work. A person has to be ready and open to it."

"But I have been ready," said Ben. "I've needed it."

"We're all capable of thought transference," said Mr. Osenko. "We all need it. Some of us are even ready. But open to it is another thing. That requires a particu-

lar surrender of our own drive to cope on our own. Individuality and separateness of the spirit is good. But
none of us can make it on our own."

"Which is what part of me has been trying to do,"
admitted Ben.

"We all want to be heroes," said Mr. Osenko sym-
pathetically. "Unique is fine. Alone is ridiculous. It gives
each of us the feeling we can run our lives separately,
which is the same thing as feeling we can control our
own small universe, which is the same thing as feeling
in a sneaky sort of way we can run the whole show.
End of lecture. You're doing fine, now. Let's cope."

Ben had been alone so long, he was nearly shaking
with relief at being able to communicate with someone
at last. Mr. Osenko was right. Learning to be a whole
self was good. It was a necessary strength against be-
coming passive. But any further strength came from simply acknowledging the thought that we're all linked together and not on our own at all. Especially when the
going got rough.

"Will you *please* for once leave the analysis for
later," came Mr. Osenko's firm thought pattern.

"Sorry," Ben conveyed in return. "Shut up and listen, yes?"

"Yes," confirmed Mr. Osenko.

That mental telepathy was possible was less of a
surprise to Ben than something else. The gentle but absolutely persuasive capacity that Mr. Osenko had that
enabled him to make another mind, Ben's own, function

at its own individual best, to the fullest of its own capacity. It was a fully free, nondominating exchange. In return, Ben had to train out of himself certain character defects of his own that stood in the way of full communication, any areas of stubborness, arrogance, impatience, resistance.

Mr. Osenko spent several days teaching Ben's mind to exercise his telepathic power.

It was then up to Ben to complete the task with the light, since Mr. Osenko, as an adult, could not confront the light himself.

"I don't fully understand the process, but it's in accord with your vision of the light when it altered form. It's definitely a matter of wanting only the young and is strongly resistant to the powers of adults. But you should reach it more completely using its own form of communication. And you may also be able to reach some of your friends."

Ben decided two things had to be done simultaneously. He had to go on trying to decrease the power of the light by the method he had already been using. He had also to begin seducing his friends away from the light and into the repossession of their own minds and lives with this newly developed telepathic power. And neither would be easy.

Although it had been necessary for Ben to spend time with Mr. Osenko to gather strength, nearly each day there had been a distinct red streak from the black night sky down toward the island. Ben knew that with each infusion the orb was gaining strength, too.

Each arming for combat once more. Time to fight now, with everything in his mind, until either he won— or the power from whatever the light's sources of power simply took over and absorbed the Earth.

"Only one of you can be Pied Piper in this story," confirmed Mr. Osenko. "And you've not only got to stop the ones still here from being absorbed, you've got to pipe the others back, the ones the orb is studying. That is, if it's still possible. We don't know what the process is."

"That settles the 'what comes first' problem." Ben agreed with Mr. Osenko's thought. "I'm going back to the island."

He sailed the Pelican across the lake with little interference, his mind alert and intense, attempting to communicate his new power to the orb, to threaten it even at a distance. He made it to the beach. Through the forest. To the pool. And down.

The light had changed.

It was strong again, as Ben had thought it would be, and throbbing with life. But for the first time, it seemed to have no choice but to communicate fully with Ben. Forced by Ben's new power to transmit and receive thought patterns, the light could no longer hide and evade, it had to play Ben's game.

Ben understood all this immediately. He sat in his usual place at the bottom of the pool, crosslegged, to face, at his usual distance, the huge moon of pulsing light.

"Okay," he said calmly. "You're on."

The light began its fight to conquer Ben, not with thoughts at first, but visions. To enchant, to seduce, to conquer.

Ben was hypnotized.

With visions of all the things the minds in the orb of light knew, had seen, as they traveled endless spaces of time, visions of the far reaches of the Universe Ben had often dreamed of, the distances the alien minds seemed to be offering in exchange for something here on Earth. He was hypnotized with visions of the beautiful colors of the stars, red giants, blue giants, yellow suns, white dwarfs. Of supernova explosions, brilliant gas explosions like the Crab Nebula, of galactic collisions, whole galaxies like the Milky Way colliding in space, of interstellar gas clouds. Of the birth and death of stars and planets. Of the whole spectrum of quasars, pulsars, galactic clusters—of all the Universe is made of.

And visions also of other civilizations in his own Milky Way Galaxy, where his own Earth revolved around its own star. Strange visions, some of creatures based on other elements, developed in ways and shapes totally different—plantlike civilizations where the plants not only grew but moved; cultures formed of pure brain life, bodiless, floating around their own planets in a magnetic field, not anchored to their planet's surface by a heavier gravity. And then a vision of a civilization that might originally have been the orb's own before, for whatever reason, the minds were dispersed into space, of forms shaped of light and shadow, dissolving, altering, in a sea of dense fog illuminated with tiny, darting points of phosphorescence.

For several hours the orb kept Ben entranced by the visions of other worlds, other lives, insights not only into Earth's own galaxy, but into a vast expanse of galaxies beyond. Ben's mind was spun, rushed gloriously into all time and space. He knew then the beauty and the freedom and the knowledge these invading minds gave in exchange for absolute submission to their power.

And then, suddenly, came the warning instinct. "No, stop it, fight it. Don't let them get away with using their weapon. Use the best weapon Earth's humanity has developed, words!"

Ben struggled to get his head together, and though unspoken, words burst from his mind.

"I don't know what you think you're going to accomplish on Earth with your visions and promises, but there are a lot of people like me on this planet who don't make a habit of surrendering."

"You will, they will," said the orb silently, forced by Ben to shift its own visual weapon. Its thoughts came verbally now across the dense substance of the pool, minds into mind. And the thoughts came on youthfully seductive, as enchanting as the visions. "Where we come from doesn't matter, another galaxy somewhere, another time, past or future. We hardly remember ourselves exactly where or when, only that our minds have been floating endlessly together in collective communities of energy that you see as white orbs in space. We live in freedom from the limitations of time, the diseases of mind and body, war, competition, all the things we have learned that plague your Earth. We have been studying you, you know. Actually," and there was a glint of humor in the voice now, "many of your speculations about us were quite right."

"Terrific," responded Ben's mind. "Would you like to sort some of them out for me?"

There was laughter and echoed laughter. "Some," answered the lead voice in the orb silently. "It is true that we have drained your minds and bodies for energy for ourselves, a complicated process I won't explain now. It is true that, in your conception of it, we are our own form of laboratory and that we have both entered your minds and absorbed some of you fully into us in order to study your race not only biologically but to understand the contents of your brains. One of your psychologists, Carl Jung, was quite right when he said every mind contains its own entire racial history all the way back to its own watery beginnings, its development from the single cell to sea creatures to land creatures to *homo sapiens.* In you the memories are subconscious, but we have ways of learning all you know that you aren't aware of knowing, all the influences in your history that have made you the way you are."

"Fascinating," Ben communicated wrily, and he was fascinated, but it was not enough. "Would you mind getting to the bottom line? Why are you so interested in us?"

"Simple," answered the orb. "We are tired, and you suit us. We wish to inhabit your bodies. Young ones, of course. They will last longer. But it's a good trade, to use your vocabulary. You will have peace and health."

"And you will have us!" Ben bombarded back. "Peace and health and freedom are obviously a great deal, but the price is too high. What you're really suggesting is psychological dictatorship in return for being a kind of unthinking, unfeeling robot. The answer is *no*," said Ben. "We'll find those things our own way, not by hosting you as parasites."

Ben made an effort to get closer to the light, to test its powerful physical abilities. Still too strong. The orb preferred distance, wouldn't let him budge. Ben got the idea that body closeness disturbed the light, so he kept trying to edge forward. So far it was no use. The light's mental voice just went on talking. "Our minds are greater than yours, with far greater powers. We have been planning this for a length of time beyond your comprehension, searching for a solar system, a planet, a civilization of people we could adapt ourselves to. What makes you think you can stop our—"

"Conquest?" Ben interrupted.

"Shall we say—invitation—to a higher order of existence?"

"Shall we say being *absorbed, digested, swallowed alive*. And shall we say, forget it!" Ben kept his anger down. If he had to cope with his own anger, he would have less energy left to cope with the light. Make the light spend its energy, he felt, make it go on giving out. "Go on," urged Ben.

The youthful ego of the light took over, showing off, unable to resist its own sense of superiority. "Your silly ideas are nothing compared to our knowledge. You grow old and die; you destroy each other. We have existed millions of years longer than you, but we remain young, no wars, no conflicts, no drive, only complete pleasure, peace. We are a combined form, many forms, of pure energy directed by a central thought, a central power that energizes us all so that we can help one another, reinforce one another. We are able to make ourselves visible by light, able to travel through all space in all galaxies, so we can be one, so we can communicate, so we can exchange solar systems when suns die, explode, overexpand, give out. Without our knowledge, our ability to travel, you on Earth will die."

Ben communicated nothing. The orb went on without pause.

"We find your resistance strange. You don't seem to take easily to group thinking. You are very difficult. We don't understand entirely yet why you don't welcome our superior abilities. You fool with the beginnings of space travel. It will only be a matter of time before you discover that no mechanical space ship will ever go fast enough, that your sun will destroy you sooner than the five billion years you think now. You will eventually discover our use of telekinesis, the use of your minds—

and Earth minds are as capable as any others—to transport your bodies. You'll be able one day to use the part of your brains that knows unconsciously even now how to use this power. But with us here, you don't have to wait, don't have to worry that you may not learn these things in time to save yourselves. As I say, you are very difficult. Others of us in other parts of your planet report the same thing."

Ben thought the voice of the orb sounded more tired at the end of that speech, as if it were finding its verbal task difficult, as if it were, as he hoped, giving off energy without taking any in.

He made the mistake of trying to edge closer again.

And succeeded in instantly alerting the light to his tactical shift.

The light vibrated a distinct smile.

"In your own words, forget it!" The orb paused. "And you can forget David and Janie and the others we've already got, too, unless you're willing to cooperate a little more."

"We want them back," said Ben, anger escaping him at last.

"You think?" retorted the orb. "Here's one last sight for you."

A vision of Athens flashed in Ben's mind. He saw, on the lawn of the Jordan home, Anne and Hugo in the last stage of transformation before the final dissolution into pure light.

10 : Minds

The orb had visibly regained the energy it had just lost. There had been no red streak. Its renewed energy had had to have come from the drain on Anne and Hugo.

Ben got himself away from the pool and the island and back across the lake in a hurry. It was dawn, gold and pink clouds between the mountains, as he sailed the lake, tacking cleanly into the wind, passing one island and another, knowing all of them so well, each pine and beech tree against the sky, each rocky shore. He was glad still to be aware of these. It kept his body rooted against the flying apart of his mind.

When he got to the part of the Jordan lawn near the rose garden where he had seen the vision of Anne and Hugo, only Anne was there.

"Has he gone?"

Anne nodded.

"And are you nearly ready?"

But Ben could see that for himself. She wore a pale, flowered robe that flowed to the grass and a garden hat so that only her hands and part of her face were visible. Her skin shimmered, nearly transparent, nearly pure light.

"There is no point in our staying," said Anne. Her long sleeves, the skirt of her robe fluttered in the breeze of early morning. "Whatever the light wants us for, we give it gladly. We get so much in return. We'll all be restored, Ben. Don't worry. The light promises that."

Ben had a sour view of the light's promises, and an even more sour view of its methods—locating the pain in a human brain in order to take advantage of each individual weakness.

"There was even less point in Hugo waiting than me."

"Why have you stayed behind then?" Ben asked, knowing as he always had that the ultimate choice lay not with the orb but in themselves. Simply, if he could resist, they all could. There was nothing intrinsically special in himself but an *attitude about himself.* If only he could make Anne give him time to talk, to change the thing in herself that made her want to give in. Especially now that he could reach her telepathically. And he felt confident he could. The light itself had prepared the way for that. If only he could think of the right words to reverse anything negative in her to everything positive. She would fight then, fight like he was fighting. "Talk to me," said Ben.

"I used to think it was my being crippled that made the orb pick me first and use me to bring the others," said Anne. "And then I thought the orb might not choose me to be inhabited, might leave me out, because I was crippled. I mean, I thought it was my foot that was the weakness the orb found."

"And now?" asked Ben.

They moved, slightly apart, toward the roses. Anne bent toward the scent, and Ben was glad that some small Earth pleasure still held beauty and meaning for her. Eternity was an exquisite thought, but he hoped they would experience it as themselves, not as part of an alien mentality, and that before Eternity, they would live their lives.

"And now?" he repeated, bending over her.

"Now I know it was another weakness the orb saw." Anne's laugh was silvery. "It was the way I love you. You know how I hate being dependent on anyone, needing anyone. Part of me was very glad to give up those feelings, to be free of them."

Anne began to look confused, and in her confusion began to telepathize her thoughts. "I don't know, Ben. Everything is so simple when I feel close to the orb. When something draws me back toward you, and I have to think about my feelings again, it isn't as comfortable or as peaceful any more."

"It isn't human to be absolutely comfortable and peaceful all the time. That's dead, not alive," he telepathized back. "Anyway, it might be fun to explore our feelings about each other and think of them as strengths, not weaknesses. How about thinking of it as an adventure instead of a struggle?" He smiled down at her. "How about right now drumming up some of those positively enthusiastic ideas you used to have about me?"

Anne tilted her face up and smiled back, sending her thoughts with her smile, under a fluttering of eyelashes. "You'd have to promise not to interfere with my reading," she communicated demurely, one of their familiar jokes.

"Go on talking," Ben said. "Anne, talk to me in words, Earth's words, even if you use telepathy. Stay close to human things, use human tools. Talk to me in words, Anne. I love you. Tell me in words that you love me."

Anne was silent altogether.

"Talk about staying behind, Anne. You could have gone with Hugo. Talk about your feelings, about you and me. Tell me why you didn't go."

"I wanted to say goodby," answered Anne, speaking out loud without thinking. "To say I love you, Ben."

"And?"

"And I can't. I won't leave you."

Ben talked, out loud now, made Anne talk out loud because it seemed more real, more solid, and that was what was needed, he saw. Whatever knowledge and power he had gained he used toward one end—to make another mind strong, independent, to be all it could be, to believe in itself, to *realize itself*. Anne began to go on and on, explaining herself, making herself real once more, a person who was important because she was she.

He said little himself, only here and there an encouraging sound, a reflection of what Anne herself was discovering about herself.

And as he watched, Ben saw Anne's skin begin to take substance again; it was working. Suddenly she grew very quiet, breathed deeply, and smiled. She didn't come toward him, but walked away then, to be by herself. For a moment Ben was uncertain as to whether she had found enough strength to release herself, and then he knew. Like lightning, the familiar red streak flashed in the sky.

The orb had needed an infusion of strength again. The only reason possible was that Ben had succeeded in removing the first of its conquered minds. It was matter of using the same technique that had first been successful against the light, the "I" of the human mind against the collective "we," the strength of independence against the weakness of the undifferentiated. And the tool was the one humans knew best—words.

He trusted that Anne was all right, that it was all right to leave her and move on. He had to reclaim his other friends now, those who were still left to reclaim. Those who would give him the opening Anne had finally given him, in order to begin. But at least now he had the key. And he could reach even minds that resisted on the surface, with telepathy.

On whose mind should he begin? Find Lakey, he

thought. Of those left, she was the most undefended. If Ben could help her find some deeper part of her human self, she would have the strength to resist the way Anne had. Loving the self. Loving others without total dependency. Keep those things in front, thought Ben, knowing where to find Lakey and going there.

He went to Athens' bar, where Lakey, twisted by the light, did sad things to herself with men. Ben was nearly eighteen, he was well known, the bartender gave him no trouble. He sat at the bar in the dim room and ordered beer. He drank it slowly, watching Lakey in one of the booths. Her eyes were blank, her mouth fixed in an inviting smile, waiting for a man, any man to drift in. Less transformed than most of the others, Lakey's skin glowed less obviously. Was she less interesting to the orb as a carrier? Had she some inner area of resistance, that once bubbling vitality, that made her cling to her own humanness more sturdily?

She saw Ben, but gave no signal. She didn't want him interfering with business. There was only one way, then, that Ben could get to her.

Do business. He moved from his bar stool toward her booth.

He leaned over and placed a twenty dollar bill on the table in front of Lakey.

Her eyes filled. "You, Ben?" was all she said. But she got up from the booth and followed him from the bar.

He led her out of town into a clearing near the

stream he used to fish in when life had been normal, a long time ago.

When he stood still to indicate they were where he wanted them to be, Lakey glanced briefly at him, hurt, and suddenly began to undress.

"No," Ben said aloud.

As with Anne, Ben alternated spoken words with telepathic words, using the power of his own self to help Lakey define herself. When for a moment, Lakey fought back with the galactic visions the orb had shown her, made her long for, Ben countered with a vision of what her life could be like living it herself on Earth, but the vision worked less well than words.

"You," Ben kept repeating, "what matters is your surviving as *you*. Find your own forever, Lakey, don't be part of someone else's. Survive, Lakey, or you'll be no good to anyone. Least of all yourself."

"No good at all," murmured Lakey. "And I want to be good for something, Ben. I do."

Her protests slipped occasionally back into the orb's line, and Ben repeatedly stopped her short, made her define herself verbally. Then, as he knew it would, an invisible line was crossed. As Lakey retrieved herself, drew a deep breath, relaxed, another red streak flashed from the sky.

He found Jimmy and Michael in the school swimming pool, Michael watching as Jimmy dove, swam, angled like a fish under water, doing lap after lap. It was like a womb in the swimming pool enclosure, heated, moist, echoing in the blue-green emptiness that smelled of chlorine.

Ben held his breath for a moment against what he had to do, the effort, the necessary control of his own self. He fought then, with a power that had increased since it had worked with Anne and Lakey, to free their minds from the orb, together and then separately. Beginning once more with telepathy, but words, not visions, he drew them slowly back to Earth. When he had done all he could, he left the pool and went outside the school building.

Another red streak. Victory, if it was final. It was a point he wasn't sure of yet, the finality. It seemed to be true that in freeing their minds, they repossessed their bodies, that the orb's ability to take over bodies required entrance through the mind first. What Ben couldn't know were the parameters of the orb's abilities, how complete it's knowledge was of human functions, it's knowledge of anything. It was always possible, as Ben fought in one direction that the orb might find another.

And he was tiring. He needed rest. Later on perhaps Anne, Lakey, Jimmy, and Michael would help him with the others.

And with the two remaining tasks: finding a way to bring the others back, the ones it had already taken, to make the orb release them intact from whatever condition they were in now; and destroying, finally, the power of the orb.

But that would have to be later.

When Ben woke in the deepening afternoon, there was an unaccustomed stillness. As if while he had been sleeping, there had been a shift in atmosphere, in the forces that battled over Athens. He felt strangely unclear, less able to think, to plan. The fear he had had before he slept reoccurred to him, that the minds in the orb, the computerlike leader, had found a newer, swifter process.

"Have you seen Mr. Osenko, ma?" Ben asked. He drank gratefully the hot chocolate his mother handed to him. The autumn afternoons were growing colder now.

"Haven't seen him all day. He's in his room, as far as I know. It's not like him, though, not to come down for his cup of tea about this time," said Mrs. Donald.

Ben climbed the stairs of the darkened old house to the third floor to find Mr. Osenko's door slightly ajar. Ordinarily, he would have knocked, but there was something about the atmosphere today that resisted sound, and very quietly, Ben pushed the door open.

At first he saw nothing in the dim room, jumbled with piles of books and Mr. Osenko's strewn possessions, barely lit by a small lamp in the far corner.

And then he saw Mr. Osenko. He lay on his bed, pale and colorless, as if everything had been drained from him, but not willingly like the others—against his will. Because he had ventured too far with his telepathy, perhaps? Or was he fighting, too, somehow. Holding off the power while Ben slept. A red streak shot through the sky, and Ben hurried out.

He went for Anne, no time for the others, and they piled into the boat. The shock of seeing Mr. Osenko forced Ben to think again, to plan. On the way to the long island, he explained what he thought had happened, what he thought he saw, what he thought the orb's new tactic was.

"I think it's simple," said Ben. "I think he was trying to help—he found a way to reach something. But they're holding him, keeping him. Studying him to find a way to defeat me, because he broke through and helped me."

Anne looked frightened. "Your mother, Ben! She helped didn't she?"

"She's not telepathic," Ben said, trying to hope.

And then he explained to Anne, as they neared the long island, what he was going to do.

"You can't," whispered Anne. "You can't do it." She telepathized her worry.

"Talk out loud, use words," Ben said. "It seems stronger here. And let's come about. Grab the mainsail. I'll take the tiller now."

They moved carefully in the boat, adjusting positions, Ben keeping Anne occupied for the moment so she would worry less, communicate her worry less to the almost tangibly extended power around them.

"I wish I knew, I wish I could still receive and understand, so I could know the orb's reaction to what you just said. But I can't be sure the way I used to be, because I'm no more plugged in than you are any more."

Ben smiled, glad beyond measure to see Anne's skin reflect the moonlight rather than glow with a light of its own, to see her eyes alert instead of blank, to see the healthy hands work the boat instead of flutter in the wind.

"Thank God you're not plugged in," said Ben.

"So how come that's exactly what you plan to do? You know what can happen if you surrender to the orb. It can change you so you won't be able to function at all, much less do what you said you're going to do."

"If we destroy the orb now, we'll never get the others back. I don't know why, but I'm certain of that. A lot of this process is psychic, but a lot is physical, too. The fact remains, that they have got the others, their bodies, not just their minds. The ones still in town might automatically reverse if the orb were destroyed, but not the ones they've got in the orb at the bottom of the pool. No, we've got to do it this way, Anne. I'll surrender in exchange for the others, and I'll hope that, thinking that once they've got me, they'll assume they can always get the others back. I'm counting on the strength of the "I" in me to fight back after I've surrendered just long enough to get what we want. And I'm counting on you. Jimmy and Michael and Lakey, but mostly on you, to help will me back. You'll have to concentrate, keep the connection between us. Give me strength."

"I'm nervous," said Anne wrily. "I'll do it, but I'm nervous."

"Yeah," said Ben.

"Under the circumstances," said Anne, "I wonder why I don't find 'yeah' the most comforting of all remarks."

They crept through the forested island. The darting lights, the turbulence of the pool looked more menacing than ever that night. But they got where they wanted to go, and slipped into the density, shuddered briefly at the level of pain, and found themselves quickly at the bottom facing the huge white orb once more.

"So we've got you at last," the orb conveyed simply.

Ben lowered his head in submission, but said, "Only if you promise to let the others out."

"And her?" came the vibration.

"Not her," returned Ben.

"It doesn't matter. With you, we'll have them all sooner or later. Go now, back later." Ben could almost feel the youthful, arrogant shrug of assurance. And the crafty smugness in the orb's next message. "You saw Mr. Osenko? You understand what we can do?"

Ben felt an instant rush of anger, of fear at what lay ahead.

The instant passed and he moved, was allowed to move, toward the light.

11 : Beyond the Light

The nearer Ben was drawn to the orb, the more his senses altered. He was chilled, his body temperature seemed lower. He understood why the others had dressed more warmly. As his skin began to glow, to grow phosphorescent, there was an accompanying feeling of lightness, and as the change in his body matter was converted to light, he felt very nearly weightless. The density of the pool's atmosphere steadied him, and he understood also why his friends had seemed languid, slow to move. It was especially hard to move his facial muscles, which would account for the blankness of their expressions.

Despite the physical conversion, Ben still felt his ultimate control. The orb's power depended on the absolute surrender of the will, and Ben's surrender depended upon the exchange.

He halted, exerting his own pull against the light,

and waited in the looming, white glare. The orb transmitted no thought patterns, but its pulsations altered and there were vague alterations in the center of its substance, the movement of forms shaping and reshaping.

"Well?" Ben transmitted his impatience.

A vibration much like a huge sigh reached him, and the orb began to emit the forms it had shaped, white forms of light, one after the other. They drifted, weightless, at a distance from Ben, across the dim bottom of the pool toward Anne, nearly a dozen of them. As they drifted, they took on substance, their luminescence dimming, their faces and bodies solidifying into the familiar structures of Hugo, David and Janie, Susan, Jake, the others. All the missing were accounted for, and Ben waited, counting them, until, led by Anne, they had disappeared upward toward the surface of the pool. The support of their thoughts reached him, and he hoped they would reach him where he was going.

Alone, himself against the mind leader again, Ben faced the light.

"Well," breathed the orb, completing the transaction.

Ben aquiesced, surrendering at last to the magnetic pull, to the enemy he had fought for so long.

It seemed forever, floating across that last space toward the orb, looming large, white, powerful before him, its rhythmic pulsations strong and hypnotic. Toward the last, he felt very little physical sensation at all, in part because his body functions were disoriented. Words, thoughts, emotional reactions seemed disconnected, as if wires had been cut and he couldn't put things together very properly now. It was almost a feeling of absolute free-float, as an object drifting in seawater.

There wasn't any one moment when he entered the light. He became light, was absorbed by the light, lost form and shape inside the great ball, although whatever particles he was clung together so that, structureless, he was still Ben. As his body patterns had dissolved, so had his mental patterns, but his thoughts, like the physical particles, revolved around each other rather than drifting away. Angers, panics, loves, plans, long-forgotten chemistry formulas, his rock under the pine trees—all were there. His unique identity remained. But like the pieces of a clock taken apart, nothing functioned in any way he was used to.

"The others felt pretty disorganized, too," came the voice of the orb. "Scattered, I believe, was the word Jake used. Far out was Susan's description."

"Sounds like Susan," said Ben. "Now what?"

"Now we do battle on our ground," answered the lead voice, with a chorus of murmured agreement from the other orbiting minds. "Now we smooth out your differences, like your Earth sea does to pebbles on the sand, until you are just like all others, until your precious identity, your self, as you call it, doesn't exist any more and you become part of us, our mind, not singularly your own. Then one of us will study your physiology, as the others were studied, so that we can comfortably inhabit your mind and body and live in you on your planet."

Ben felt the sensation of a projected smile as the lead voice continued, "In this case, me. I have chosen you, Ben."

"Gratifying," responded Ben from some thought pattern that still responded. The weapon of words had been removed along with his dissolution.

The bombardment was begun with the orb's best weapon, visions. Visions meant to make him feel the smallness of himself, but in the beginning the orb chose the wrong vision.

Ben saw himself standing on a long, pale ribbon of beach at dawn, watching the sunrise over an endless sea. For Ben it had always been the most quiet, the most awesome time, because it was then he felt, understood, the vastness of the production, that it wasn't for him, that it wasn't simply a natural expected morning phenomenon of the Earth, but a revelation of the vast working of the Universe. He saw the sun then as part of the immensity of things, huge as it truly was, not simply its relative size in his human mind, but in its full enormity, and not just the sun itself, but all the other suns beyond in the overwhelming extension of all space. What the orb couldn't have known, permitting Ben this vision, was that while it made his outsides feel small, a speck in time and place, it made his insides feel big, knowing that he was a part, an unloseable, identifiable part, of the vast production of Eternity.

The orb calculated the effect on Ben quickly,

changed the vision. This time, the vision was more violent. There was a sudden whirling that Ben felt could be disastrous to his already minimal connections to the various parts of himself. And then he was a part of space itself. He saw clearly the fiery mists of Sagittarius, with its swarms of suns that hid the heart of the galaxy. He saw the dark black shadow of the Coal Sack, the hole in space where no stars shone.

The orb was reminding Ben, truly teaching him, the miracle of movement through space in the form of light—and was hoping, again, to teach Ben something else, something of its own. That, joining the light, he could be part of that miracle. And again, that Ben was small, undifferentiated from all other specks in the Universe.

Only again, it didn't work. To Ben, the smallest part was the same as the largest part, a part of the whole. And it served, this vision, only to reinforce his sense of himself as a unique part. There was still only one Ben, one speck that saw, felt, thought, exactly as he saw, felt, thought; had from the beginning, and would until the end, if there were a beginning or an end. He felt an ecstasy of the self, not a division from it, an absolute integrity, not a fragmentation. With all the disconnection the orb was trying to effect in Ben, he was only growing stronger.

"Once you accept yourself as part of Forever," Ben had once said to Anne, "nothing can destroy you."

It was true! He was proving it was true.

"You are stubborn, selfish, and spoiled," communicated the orb suddenly. "And you're being difficult."

"Yes," Ben agreed with a great deal of pleasure. He was back in the orb's white center again, feeling as if he were under a large, undefined microscope being examined by a hundred pair of eyes.

"You have begun to feel a little more connected than when you first came into us. We can very easily scramble you again, you know."

"Time," thought Ben, trying desperately to block his own thought from the orb's intent examination. "And in that instant he felt something else resisting the light, something reaching out to him from beyond. Anne? Lakey? Jimmy, Michael, maybe even some of the rest? He could keep together on his own, but he couldn't get back on his own.

Could the ones outside make a bridge, a thought bridge before he got sent off into another vision again? Ben concentrated on his friends as hard as he could. Reached toward their minds, their caring.

In the fervor of his attempt he tried to shut what there was of himself off from the light to protect himself. He all but stopped thinking, desperately reaching. He had resisted the dissolution of his identity, but he had only so much energy. Other than remaining himself, he could do no more.

He could feel the orb's forces transmitting at him, he could feel their power trying to weaken, to disconnect him, to cut him off from himself, from anyone on

Earth, to scramble him completely.

But the outside force was also growing stronger. It was as if opposing forces were battling for his scattered particles.

There were sensations, finally, of pulling, of being lifted, of being flung out again, this time not among the stars, but into the familiar density of the bottom of the pool.

Ben really came together in Mr. Osenko's room. His friends took him there, because he felt it would be a place of healing, if Mr. Osenko were still there. If he was not dead, or gone.

The old teacher, philosopher, friend was sitting in his chair. He was still, too tired to speak or think, but the serenity of his smile was touched with humor. And seeing that, Ben felt a new kind of peace, a peace the light would never have understood, flooding over him, restoring his energy, giving him rest. It was so, then, what the two of them had often debated. The cosmos wasn't founded on tragedy, but joy.

"Thank you," said Ben. Aloud. In words. And Mr. Osenko nodded.

Anne was waiting for Ben when he came to her house that evening.

"Are the others all right, Hugo, David, Janie, the rest?" said Ben, touching her hands, her face, grateful to find her flesh solid, normal like his own.

"Yes," whispered Anne. "We're all fine. It's done, Ben. Everyone's all right. You won." She paused. "Do you suppose, if it's happened other places, they've won, too?"

"I would think," said Ben. "We're all made of the same stuff."

"Did you think they were bad?" asked Anne.

"No," said Ben, laughing. "Just different. And I like it better our way."

"One more," said Anne. "Will they try again?"

Ben stared briefly up into the night toward the Milky Way. "They may. But so will we."

They went down to the dock then and readied the Pelican as they talked, both wanting urgently to get to the island. Anne took the tiller as Ben raised the sails. Together they sailed the old way across the silent lake and beached the boat. And they went along the accustomed path to the pool.

They stood dazed at its edge. For months, since last June, they had seen there a blue-white luminescence, darting lights, strangely shifting, turbulent waters, felt the pull from beneath.

Tonight, the water was dark, calm, simple as it had been all the years before. They knelt down, let their hands drift to feel the lake's substance. Water. Nothing dense, nothing extraordinary. Water, and it was October, cold.

But Ben couldn't stand not knowing absolutely. He stripped down to his shorts and dove in.

Still, just water. He couldn't breathe it, it wasn't an atmosphere he could live in. He went as far down as he could, as before, not able to touch bottom. Nowhere was there a light. Nowhere did he feel the tug, the seductive power. It was gone. Whatever had been was gone.

He went back to Anne, shivering as he surfaced and pulled on his clothes. The night was dark, calm, as they stood there close.

"It's over," she breathed.

But a slight furtive movement of her hand sent a strange electric shudder through Ben's body. He reached quietly for her hand, and in the darkness of the island forest turned her wrist upward. He saw what he had hoped never to see again. It was pale, but it was there: the faint impression of the luminescent patch.

They both saw it before Ben covered it with his own hand. And they both had the same lingering thought. Was that faint light on Anne's arm still a connecting link? Did it mean that Anne was still part of that world of light minds drifting through space, that she could draw them back or they draw her to them?

They didn't look again at the mark of the orb.

For now, there were no more answers.

For now, there was only now.

And with the stars in their place, and Ben and Anne in theirs, it was, quite simply, a beautiful October night.